SHAIHU UMAR

SHAIHU UMAR

na

Alhaji Sir Abubakar Tafawa 'Balewa

SHAIHU UMAR

a novel by
Alhaji Sir Abubakar Tafawa Balewa

Translated with a forward
for the English edition
by
MERVIN HISKETT
University of London

Introduction for the
first American edition
by
BEVERLY B. MACK
George Mason University

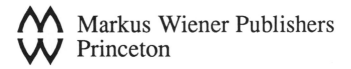 Markus Wiener Publishers
Princeton

First American edition published by Markus Wiener Publishers in 1989.
Second printing, 1994.
Third printing, 1996.
Fourth printing, 2000.
Fifth printing, 2006

For information write to:
Markus Wiener Publishers
231 Nassau Street, Princeton, NJ 08542
www.markuswiener.com

Library of Congress Cataloging-in-Publication Data

Balewa, Abubaker Tafawa, Sir, 1912-1966.
    Shaihu Umar.
    (Topics in World History)
    Translation of: Shaihu Umar.
    I. Hiskett, M.   II. Title.   III. Series
    PL8234.B3S513   1989   893'.723   89-5765
    ISBN-13: 978-1-55876-006-6
    ISBN-10: 1-55876-006-7

Markus Wiener Publishers books are printed in the United States of America on acid-free paper, and meet the guidelines for permanence and durability of the Committee on Production Guidelines for Book Longevity of the Council on Library Resources.

Introduction to the American Edition of
Shaihu Umar
BY BEVERLY B. MACK
GEORGE MASON UNIVERSITY

The publication of Sir Abubakar Tafawa Balewa's novel *Shaihu Umar* in 1955 was an immediate success among Hausa speakers in Northern Nigeria, who considered the author their spokesman and hero. It was reprinted in Hausa six times by 1976, and continues to be popular as a work exemplary of traditional Hausa culture and the Islamic values with which it has been infused. In 1967 it was translated into the English form that appears here, and immediately went into a second printing the following year. The production of a film of *Shaihu Umar* in 1970 and a play of the same name by Umaru Ladan and Dexter Lyndersay testifies to its continued popularity.

The story's enduring appeal is immediately evident as the title character is introduced as an honorable man: ". . . there was once a certain malam, learned in the stars, in the Koran, and in the scriptures, and an upholder of the Faith. This malam was one of the men of the world to whom God has given the gift of knowledge. His name was Shaihu Umar." From such a classic beginning, the story segues into less orthodox excitements of kidnapping, slave-raids, caravans crossing the Sahara, intrigues, death, destruction, abandonment, and exotic adventure in West and North Africa. It is a parable of goodness triumphing over evil, and fortitude in the face of hardship. The book is an entertainment that presents the history of Northern Nigeria at the turn of the century, without ever seeming like a history lesson. The remembrance that comprises the story begins placidly enough, with Shaihu Umar in Nigeria, reminiscing about his origins: "Away back I was a native of this country, but even so, I did not grow up and pass my boyhood here. It was far away in the country of the Arabs that I grew up." As with any good tale, the adventure lies in the journey; how he got there and back is the exciting part. Before the story is finished, Umar has been kidnapped several times, captured as a slave, given to an Arab who takes him to Egypt, and finally set free to make his way home and find his mother before she dies. Through it all he becomes a respected and revered scholar and religious man, whose fame spreads far and wide.

Along the way the reader discovers a great deal about Hausa history and culture, philosophy and values, expressed in the character of the men and women who populate the tale. These are people who live in a time when "civil war raged, slave raiding was rife, and life for the common people was dangerous and miserable" (*West Africa,* December 16, 1967, p. 1608). Despite this, traditional Hausa values and the code of ethics inspired by orthodox Islam buoy them, and good character triumphs in the face of tribulation.

The story's author is remembered as just such a man of good character. He was a teacher of humble origins who rose to importance as a significant political figure in Nigeria's transition from British overrule to independence, leaving a literary, as well as political, legacy to his country.

HAUSA ORIGINS

The West African region known as Hausaland comprises approximately the northern half of Nigeria and the southern edge of Niger, with its heart lying in the north central area of present-day Nigeria. For centuries Hausaland has been the focus of legend and a center of trade and cosmopolitan society.

Some of its cities, like Kano and Katsina, have been major cultural and commercial centers since the fifteenth century.

The Hausa people now share a common language and culture, but among their antecedents are migrant hunter-gatherers of diverse languages and cultures who converged on the West African savannah that was to become Hausaland. Their gradual consolidation occurred prior to the tenth century, with the establishment of stable clan-oriented settlements. Legend describes these early inhabitants as smiths and fire-worshippers who were descended from Barbushe, founder of Kano, the city that was to become the heart of Hausaland. The original inhabitants of Kano are believed to have been animists, sometimes known as "pagans"; the distinction between them and Muslim immigrants became increasingly significant throughout the centuries. While some Hausa people still follow religious practices that pre-date the appearance of Islam in the region (called "arne" or pagan), most are now Muslim.

TRANS-SAHARAN TRADE AND ISLAM IN HAUSALAND

Hausaland's formation and consolidation occurred well before Islam became a cultural influence in the area, but once it was introduced, Islam's effect was pervasive, even changing the way people conducted business. Islam became a critical factor in the development of Hausaland as early as the tenth century. At first, it was a religion of the elite and royalty, who enjoyed visits from North African Muslims who were scholars, architects, poets, and other travelers. These Arab Muslims were impressive in Hausaland for their literacy and devotion to a philosophy that directed their lives.

By the early fifteenth century the area boasted great walled cities that served as the centers of kingdoms vying for control of the region. These city-centers flourished, benefitting from trans-Shaharan commerce that involved as much cultural exchange as commercial trade. In the major markets Hausa and Arabic languages, religious perspectives, and cultural philosophies were commodities as important as material goods. Hausas who could communicate with Arab traders and understood their Islamic outlook on commercial transactions stood to prosper in the Hausa markets. The integration of Islam into Hausa culture was as good for business as it was for literacy rates. Thus, Arabic culture and Islam became integral aspects of Hausa identity, and it was during this period that the city of Kano became a major economic and cultural center for sub-Saharan Africa.

Human beings continued to be a major commodity along the trans-Saharan trade routes, and Kano itself had a renowned slave market that processed a large number of slaves captured in Hausaland. This African-Arab slave trade responded to market needs in North Africa and beyond, supplying domestic labor for affluent families in Tripoli, and fulfilling the needs of Ottoman sultanates. In West Africa, local skirmishes provided a constant source of human booty, as local leaders vied for control over ever-larger areas. In addition, people often were kidnapped in the countryside. Captives were sold locally, and then transported across the desert for resale in North Africa.

As a result of trans-Saharan trade, including the slave trade, Hausaland's economy flourished in the fifteenth and sixteenth centuries. During this period, increasing numbers of Muslim Arabs streamed into Hausa cities, which were the southern trade centers of trans-Saharan caravan routes. Conversion to Islam became important for successful interaction with Arab traders, and the numbers of Hausa converts rose steadily.

Gradually Islam became a religion of the people. Cultural and economic change along increasingly trafficked trans-Saharan trade routes fostered growth and prosperity for the region. Slaves were a lucrative item for trade northward, as were salt and kola nuts. As Arab traders exchanged their Mediterranean commodities for these, they also brought literacy and Islamic practices to their counterparts in Hausaland. By the late eighteenth century, traders and migrants were preaching Islam in the savannah region of West Africa, traveling regularly along trans-Saharan caravan routes like the ones depicted in *Shaihu Umar.*

THE FULANI AND THE SOKOTO *JIHAD*

Between the fifteenth and eighteenth centuries another ethnic group, the Fulani, filtered into Hausaland from the West African coastal regions. Most were pastoralists who followed their cattle and remained in the countryside. The intellectual elite embraced Islam and became literate scholars. In this capacity they found useful positions as religious and political advisors in major Hausa royal courts like those of Kano and Katsina. As the eighteenth century drew to a close, these Fulani clerics became distressed about the persistence of both religious and secular pre-Islamic Hausa customs, especially the proclivity for song and dance. They believed that these customs were opposed to Islamic values, and therefore needed to be purged.

Tension between groups representing these two perspectives culminated in a Fulani-led campaign of reformation, or *jihad* led by Shehu Usman Dan Fodio. ("Shehu," the title for a pious learned man, is also spelled "shaihu," as in our story, and "shayk," "sheik," or "shaik.") The Shehu was a Fulani who, in the capacity of a Muslim scholar, had become embroiled in a series of disputes with a local king. The ensuing power struggle, which was perceived as a struggle for the supremacy of Islam, inspired the Shehu to rally supporters, and from 1804 to 1812 his growing bands of Fulani Muslim reformists swept over Hausaland as far east as Bornu. They conquered Hausa kings and replaced them with Fulani leaders known as emirs. This *jihad* of Islamic revival resulted in a new Fulani theocratic state, and it is in this context that *Shaihu Umar* takes place.

In nineteenth-century Hausaland, local power rivalries made internecine warfare and its attendant insecurity common features of the times; *jihad* skirmishes added to the danger of the period. Those who were not Muslim faced the prospect of being killed or captured and sold into slavery. The propagation of Islam was inextricably involved with competition for local power, and although the enslavement of fellow Muslims was forbidden in theory, nevertheless many were swept up in the struggle.

The *jihad* did not stem the tide of slaves transported to North Africa. On the contrary, in an effort to gain an emir's favor, his men often would go out on slave-raiding expeditions to capture rural peoples so their lord could sell them. It is just such a slave-raid that figures prominently in our tale. Slave-raiding also existed on a smaller scale. While he is still too young to tell where he lives, Shaihu Umar himself is kidnapped by a stranger who hopes to sell him for profit.

This, then, is the setting for *Shaihu Umar:* Islam, Arabs, slavery, and local warfare were regular features of nineteenth-century Hausaland. Non-Muslims could legally and morally be bought and sold, according to the code of the time, and were often sold into slavery. It was not unusual for caravans to carry slaves across the desert to Egypt or Tripoli, and all too common for families to be divided in such trade. Furthermore, being Muslim did not preclude involvement as an agent in the slave trade, and although the enslavement of fellow Muslims theoretically was forbidden, that was no guarantee of immunity from capture. The temptation to profit from slave sales made it all too easy to ignore a person's status as a Muslim, often on the grounds that his behavior was insufficiently orthodox.

The story begins by sketching a common situation of the time: a respectable Muslim man is first involved in slave raiding and then himself falls victim to his fellow slave-raiders. This is Umar's step-father, an upright man, who accompanies his peers on a slave-raid conducted at the bidding of the emir. He is exiled when jealous and ambitious peers, vying for their new emir's favor, frame him, saying he has cheated the emir by hiding for his own use some of the slaves he captured. Leaving town, he promises to send for his wife and child, Umar, once he is established elsewhere. But these are dangerous times, and before the family can be reunited, Umar not only loses his step-father, but is also separated from his mother when a stranger steals him at play. Before he can profit from his booty, the abductor is mauled by a hyena, and the young Umar is adopted by local farmers. However, the existence of rural folks is uncertain at best, and the family's concern for the boy's welfare is thwarted as they themselves are captured by one of the emir's men, Gumuzu. Ironically, Gumuzu is himself a slave, although of royal status and privilege; when no one will buy the little family because they have suffered too much and are in bad shape, they settle down to live with Gumuzu in Kano. One day an Arab friend visits Gumuzu before setting off to return to Egypt. Upon seeing young Umar, the Arab, Abdulkarim, asks Gumuzu to let the boy accompany him home, since he has no son of his own. Separated from guardians yet again, the boy is raised by Abdulkarim in Egypt, where he is educated as a Muslim scholar and becomes a renowned Shaihu, a pious teacher.

Through the story's twists and turns, its author emphasizes a belief that underlies Muslim Hausa philosophy: trust in God's will. Shaihu Umar never understands why life has dealt him such trials, but he is pious enough to accept his fate as it unfolds. Indeed the character of Shaihu Umar represents a revered member of Hausa society, the religious scholar, or *mallam*, whose own exemplary life inspires others. His faith in God is made more poignant by the fact that he himself has been a victim of the trans-Saharan slave trade. Shaihu Umar is sketched as a *mutumin kirki*, a "good man"; in Hausa culture this requires fortitude in the face of difficulties, faith in God, humility, generosity, and dedication to hard work.

AUTHOR AND TRANSLATOR

This description of the "good man" also fits the tale's creator, Alhaji Sir Abubakar Tafawa Balewa, one of the most significant figures in early modern Nigeria history. His several titles indicate his accomplishments in both Muslim and colonial worlds: he is called "Alhaji" for having fulfilled the journey to Mecca, one of the obligations of every Muslim, and he was granted British knighthood ("Sir") for his role as a politician and diplomat. Although he was born in 1912, just about a decade after the official abolition of slavery in Nigeria, the institution of slavery and the slave trade itself were familiar to him in early life. Born in Bauchi, a rural region of Northern Nigeria, he himself was of slave lineage, and from his parents' generation he often heard stories about the perils of rural life in a time of political competition that involved slave-raids and fostered insecurity.

It must have been an adventure for young Balewa even to travel to Katsina, in northwestern Nigeria, to attend Katsina College. After receiving his teacher's certificate there, he made a yet more daring move to London to study education at the University. Upon his return to Nigeria he served as an Education Officer, and then embarked on a political career. Named Chief Minister in 1957, he soon became a central figure in Nigerian politics, helping to orchestrate the country's transition to independence at the end of the colonial period. When

Nigeria gained its independence in 1960, Balewa became the country's first Prime Minister, and gained international recognition and respect for his dignity, fairness, and capability in shaping Nigerian policy both at home and abroad.

Balewa's political energy was focused on the country's unity and prosperity, and his loyalty to the conservative arm of established leaders involved strong support for Northerners who could promote Hausa interests. But certain factions felt that the time had come for a reallocation of power among ethnic and regional groups in the country. On January 14, 1966, Nigeria's first military coup was organized by military opponents of the established political order. It resulted in the deaths of several important figures, Balewa among them. Balewa's strong identification as a conservative Northerner representing Hausa ethnic interests marked him as a prime target, and his death at the hands of the opposition was a significant loss to the country. Today he remains revered by those who acknowledge his contributions to Nigeria's political development. Perhaps more important than his historical role as a politician, though, is his memory as an exemplary man.

Balewa never had the chance to retire and devote himself to writing and studying, but the first loves of his lifetime were teaching and upholding his culture's traditions. While the message of *Shaihu Umar* underlines Balewa's origins as a teacher, its entertaining style testifies to Balewa's literary genius. Although Balewa was not primarily an author—*Shaihu Umar* was his only major literary work, and was written while he was serving as Prime Minister—nevertheless, it continues to be one of the culture's most popular and enduring tales, taking its place among the works that form the central core of contemporary Hausa literature. It was first published in Hausa in 1955, and has been reprinted regularly since then. The first English translation, published in 1967, was reprinted immediately in 1968. Following that, a film version was produced in Hausa and distributed widely in Nigeria in the 1970s, making it accessible to the illiterate as well as students and scholars.

The literary climate that laid the foundation for the production of Balewa's novel, like the plot itself, is rooted in the nineteenth century. Prior to this time in Hausaland, Islamic poetry was written completely in Arabic, or in Hausa, transliterated into Arabic script. It was transported along the same commercial lines as slaves and other goods, across the desert by caravan. In Hausaland, *jihad* leader Shehu Usman Dan Fodio was prolific in his production of religious verse supporting his cause. He also produced works in a narrative form that became popular in the nineteenth century, the travel account. This form appealed to Hausa authors as well as European travelers. *Shaihu Umar* is influenced by these works; it was originally written in Hausa, and has been popular among schoolchildren since its first publication. As indicated in its first English introduction, *Shaihu Umar* is more than just a story; it is also an expression of the "values and philosophy of orthodox Islám," as well as a portrait of traditional African life. Its focus on morality and piety underlines the culture's overriding concern for the quality of an individual's character.

In translating this story from the Hausa and seeing it into print over twenty years ago, Professor Mervyn Hiskett opened a window for the world on traditional Hausa culture. Indeed, Hausa culture has become part of Professor Hiskett's own life. For many years he made his home in Nigeria, teaching in Kano's School for Arabic Studies early in his career and later lecturing on Hausa culture at Nigerian universities. For over twenty years he was a lecturer in Hausa Studies at the University of London's School for Oriental and African Studies, and he has published widely on a multiplicity of topics concerning Hausa history, literature, linguistics, and socio-political issues. Among his many publications are such major works as: *The Sword of Truth: The Life and Times of Shehu Usman Dan Fodio* (1973); *A History of Hausa Islamic Verse* (1975); and *The Development of Islam in West Africa* (1984). Fluent in Arabic and Hausa, Professor Hiskett studied the culture through original Arabic documents and the oral testimony of local historians. His contributions to the fields of Hausa literature, history, and cultural studies are of prime importance to scholars in many fields.

CONCLUSION

Alhaji Sir Abubakar Tafawa Balewa intended to retire from politics and devote himself to writing in his later years, but his assassination, along with that of others in the first wave of Nigeria's leadership, robbed him of the opportunity. Thus it is fitting that the man well remembered as a politician produced a literary work focused on the human spirit—a work that has outlasted his political accomplishments, and may even have eclipsed them. *Shaihu Umar* is an enduring legacy to the people and the culture he served in life and death. *Shaihu Umar* is central to an understanding of the historical and socio-economic realities of nineteenth-century Hausa culture. Captured, enslaved, freed, taken to Egypt, educated in Islam, and finally drawn back by cultural ties to Hausaland, Shaihu Umar is the epitomy of a man of his time. Furthermore, he exemplifies all that is held in esteem in Hausa culture. He is portrayed as the proverbial "good man" in Hausa culture: learned, just, disciplined, generous, and humble, deferring to the will of higher powers. The poignant saga of Shaihu Umar is timeless. It well deserves to be made available to yet another generation.

Introduction

Shaihu Umar is one of the most popular of the novels and stories written by contemporary Nigerian authors. That this should be so, is not surprising, for it is a story of great human interest. The author's account of Hausa life and institutions often implies criticism, but is always just, and is tempered by understanding. Although he has chosen the novel as his medium, his attitude is serious and thoughtful. There is no mistaking his concern about, and moral involvement in, the realities behind this tale. Beyond the criticism his belief in the human capacity for love and charity in even the most evil situation, is apparent.

The story appears at first sight to owe less to the indigenous African literary tradition than, for instance, *Gandoki*[1] or *Magana Jari Ce*,[2] and in its wholly serious approach it is poles apart from the broad and boisterous humour of *Ruwan Bagaja*.[3] But if we examine it more closely, native African life and custom are seen to underlie the whole plot. Hausa marriage custom, court life, and the institution of slavery govern the lives of Umar and his mother. The incident of the hyena[4] is an echo of the traditional animal fables in which this creature always figures, and there is a further indication of the currency of these animal tales in the reference to what the lion said to the hyena, 'Man is a thing to be feared.'[5] Moreover, throughout the story, charms, magic, and dreams constantly remind us of the magical background to African daily life. But although the African background plays an important part in this

1 By Malam Bello Kagara, Zaria, 1934
2 By Alhaji Abubakar Imam, OBE, Zaria, 1960
3 By Alhaji Abubakar Imam, OBE, Zaria, 1963
4 Page 43
5 Page 59

3

story, Islam provides the inspiration, and it is Islamic values and Muslim attitudes which mould the character of Umar and unify the plot. Indeed, *Shaihu Umar* is more than a story. It is a statement of the values and philosophy of orthodox Islam. The character of Umar is both an Islamic and a Hausa ideal. The devotion to learning, the piety and patience in adversity are part of the Hausa concept of a malam. The ideal is stated in the following passage:

'None who had studied under Shaihu Umar had ever known him impatient, nor had they ever known a day when they had come to study, and he had said that he was tired, except perhaps if he were unwell. And even if ill-health afflicted him, if it were not severe, he would without fail come out to teach. This Shaihu Umar was a man beyond all others, the like of whom is not likely to be found again. Whatever evil thing befell him, he would say, "It is God who relieves all our troubles." He never became angry, his face was always gentle, he never interfered in what did not concern him, and he never wrangled with anyone, let alone did he ever show even the slightest cantankerousness. Why, because of this character of his, it came about that in the whole country no-one ever criticised him, and many people began to say, "Certainly this is no mere man, he is a saint."'[1]

The plot of the story turns on three important Hausa institutions; the court, slavery, and the traditional Muslim system of education. The historical background to court life has been ably described by M. G. Smith in a recent article, 'Historical and cultural conditions of political corruption among the Hausa.'[2] It was an institution in which indigenous African custom had become involved with oriental and late Islamic practice, coming to the Hausa from North Africa and Bornu. Its characteristics were despotism dependent upon slavery, nepotism and intrigue. The ruler had become cut off from

1 Page 18
2 *Comparative studies in society and history*, vol. vi, no. 2, January, 1964

the common people,[1] and it was upon the courtiers and office-holders that he depended for support. He in turn controlled them through the manipulation of office and of personalities. For the courtier intrigue was the normal path to preferment, and was essential to survival. Makau's fate was simply that of any courtier who monopolised the ruler's favour and thus incurred the jealousy of his colleagues. In the scene in which Makau is confronted by the trumped-up charges,[2] Alhaji Sir Abubakar Tafawa Balewa vividly portrays this background of intrigue and jealousy.

Alongside court intrigue was the problem of judicial corruption. The author's comment upon this is implied in his account of the fate of Umar's maternal grandfather, and of his mother, who suffered so cruelly at the hands of corrupt cadis.

Towards slavery his attitude is more complex. It is clear that he is fully aware of the evils of this traffic in human beings. The constant insecurity of a society in which slaves were procured both by raiding and kidnapping is made clear to us, while the account of the slave caravan toiling across the desert, and its subsequent arrival in Ber Kufa leave us in no doubt as to the sufferings and degradation of those who fell victims to this trade. Yet there is good in men even when they are caught up in something as evil as the slave trade. Makau, while not of the moral stature of Shaihu Umar himself, conforms to the Hausa concept of *mutumin ƙirƙi*,[3] and is a kindly forgiving man who is responsibly concerned for his family and his household. Yet he takes part in a slave raid as a matter of duty, and is a slave owner. Gumuzu, himself a slave, and brutal in his capture of a peasant family, is by no means wholly evil. He has his kindly side, and his compound is not an unhappy place. Abdulkarim is of course a central figure in the story. This scholarly and dignified Arab, who is clearly capable of deep human affection and generosity, is a

1 Abdullahi, first Emir of Gwando, constantly makes the point in his famous *Diyā'
al-ḥukkām* that the greatest of all evils is that the ruler should become cut off from the people.
2 Pages 5–26
3 A good man

civilised and cultured person, and he commands our liking. Yet he makes his living as a slaver on the Saharan trade routes, and has his agent in Kano, whose job is to hunt slaves for him. Even Ahmad, who causes so much unhappiness to Umar's mother, and is finally responsible for her death, is clearly not an evil man, but simply one who is tried beyond his patience by a situation which he does not understand.

How are we to regard this apparent ambivalence? In fact, it is this which gives the story its authenticity and which makes it a convincing representation of Hausa society, and indeed of Islamic society in general, at the end of the nineteenth century. Islam permits slavery. It legislates to make it more humane and it enjoins the good treatment and manumission of slaves as religiously commendable. Basically, however, there is no doubt that it accepts slavery, and gives the master such rights over his slave as Ahmad claimed over Umar's mother. Muslim humanists, while never questioning the fundamental legality of the institution, have been concerned to humanise the traffic, and minimise the sufferings which it so clearly entailed. Indeed, it is clear that Muslims have often found themselves in a moral dilemma in that they have been fully aware of the inhumanity of an institution which, morally, they have had to accept. This dilemma is most obvious for instance, in the writings of the Timbuctu historian Ahmad Bāba, who flourished at the end of the sixteenth century.[1]

Muslim legislation governing slavery was not successful in preventing the kind of conditions which Umar witnessed on the desert crossing. But it has meant that domestic slavery has been on the whole benign, and also that the integration of the slave and of his descendants into Islamic society has been easily accomplished. Gumuzu and Umar, in their different ways, both illustrate this. It is against such a background that Sir Abubakar Tafawa Balewa

---

[1] Ahmad Bāba al-Tinbukhtī (1556–1627) wrote a work, as yet unpublished, called *al-kashf wa'l-bayān*, in which he discusses the law relating to the taking of slaves in the Sudan.

writes. This is no defence or condonement of slavery. It is a clear indictment of its evils. But it does involve an understanding of the moral and social conditions in which the characters of *Shaihu Umar* lived. It also involves the belief that human nature is never totally evil, and that good will manifest itself even when men's lives are conditioned by evil institutions.

It is clear that the author writes from his own deep knowledge of the traditional system of Muslim education as it was practised in the Western Sudan. The opening pages give a vivid impression of the master-seeking system in operation.

'In this little town there was once a certain malam, learned in the stars, in the Koran, and in the scriptures, and an upholder of the Faith. This malam was one of the men of this world to whom God has given the gift of knowledge. His name was Shaihu Umar. So great were his learning and wisdom that news of him reached countries far distant from where he lived. Men would come from other countries, travelling to him in order to seek knowledge. Before long the people coming to him foregathered, and became so numerous that they had no place to set up their compounds, so it became necessary for some of them to seek compounds in the little villages near to Rauta.'[1]

Compare this with the following passage from *Baba of Karo*:

'The men who came to study the Koran used to fill up the entrance-hut completely. They recited and recited, students from many different places, they would come with their writing-boards hung round their necks, and their womenfolk would make porridge for them to bring to us as alms. Malam Maigari was really very learned. People used to come in from the nearby villages day after day, to study under him. At dawn the men would get up and light the fire, then they would study until about 11.30 a.m. Then they ate. Then from the Azahar prayer until the La'asar prayer (2.30–5.30) they continued their discussions and reading. From the

1 Page 18

7

sundown prayer, Mangariba, until far into the night they were studying. In all that country from Kano City over towards Bornu and Hadejiya the people study a great deal, they love it.'[1]

From the account of Umar's life and schooling in Ber Kufa we learn the central part which Koran studies play in the upbringing of a Muslim boy. The successful recitation of the Koran before his masters, and the subsequent feasting are a point of high achievement by which the youth enters fully into Muslim society. Subsequent acceptance as a *shaikh* or malam is not by formal examination or appointment, but by general acclaim and consensus of opinion. The following passage describes exactly how the Muslim scholar becomes established in his own society:

'Within a few years I had come near to being the next in rank after Shaihu Mas'ud himself in the city of Ber Kufa. From that time people began to call me "Shaihu Umar", and many people from the towns of Egypt kept coming to visit me. When they came they would express astonishment, saying that here I was, a black man, and yet God had given me abundant insight and understanding. Thus I continued, and then, when Shaihu Mas'ud died, there was no doubt about it, it was I who was chosen in his place as Imam, and it was I who instructed all his students.'[2]

We may compare the account of the traditional system given in *Shaihu Umar* with that in 'Abdullāh b. Muhammad's well-known '*Idā al-nusūkh*.[3] Here he tells of the early life of Shaihu Usumanu dan Fodio:

'Then the shaikh 'Uthmān went to seek knowledge to our shaikh Jibrīl, and he accompanied him for almost a year, learning from him until he came with him to the town of Agades. Then shaikh Jibrīl returned him to his father and went on pilgrimage, for

1 Mary Smith, *Baba of Karo*, London, 1964, 131–132
2 Page 64
3 Translated by M. Hiskett, '*Material relating to the state of learning among the Fulani before their jihād*', BSOAS, xix, 3, 1957

8

('Uthmān's) father had not given him permission to go on pilgrimage.

'Now shaikh 'Uthmān informed me that he had learnt Qur'ānic exegesis from the son of our maternal and paternal uncle Ahmad ibn Muhammad ibn al-Amīn, etc., and that he was present at the assembly of Hāshim al-Zanfarī and he heard from him Qur'ānic exegesis from the beginning of the Qur'ān to the end of it. I at that time was with him, but I was not then occupied with the science of exegesis. He learnt the science of tradition from our maternal and paternal uncle al-Hājj Muhammad ibn Rāj ibn Mudibbi ibn Hamm ibn 'Āl reading with him all of the *Sahīh* of al-Bukhārī, while I listened. Then he gave us licence to pass on all that he had recited of that which he had learnt from his shaikh al-Madanī, the Sindī of origin, Abū al-Hasan 'Alī.

'In short, the shaikhs of Shaikh ('Uthmān) were many. I knew some of them, and some I did not know, and God it is who adapts affairs to the straight course.'[1]

There are other aspects of Hausa life upon which *Shaihu Umar* throws revealing light. Foremost among them is the position of women and children in the Hausa family. Marriage custom, the departure of the bride three days after the marriage ceremony, to take up her place in her husband's compound, the two-years' weaning period and subsequent bringing-up of the first child by the paternal grandmother, the function of the *kawa* or female bond-friend and the way in which the duties of mothering the children are shared to a large extent by all the women in the compound; all these are features of the Hausa scene with which we are familiar from *Baba of Karo*. They all appear as the background against which the story of Umar and his mother is set. In the same way that Umar himself represents a Hausa ideal of manhood, so his mother represents an ideal of womanhood. She defers to the authority of her husband and her own kinsfolk, yet this detracts nothing from

1 Ibid. 564

the dignity of her personality. Her position in a polygamous household is one which brings her comfort and support in her adversities; the ties of affection and kinship loyalties between herself, her husband, her own family and finally at the end of her life, her son, relieve and soften the tragedy which has afflicted her. The grace and courtesy of a young African woman in her own domestic setting are portrayed with great tenderness by the author when he describes how she receives her guests in her father's compound at Fatika.[1] Her own simple piety and the patience to which Makau and Buhari counsel her are no mere conventions. They are the source of her inner strength, at which Abdulkarim marvels.[2] Such a character as hers is an ideal, but it is not unreal, for we recognise in the living character of Baba of Karo many of the qualities with which Sir Abubakar Tafawa Balewa has so skilfully endowed this girl from Fatika.

All this certainly involves characterisation, and Sir Abubakar's concept of his characters is clear and precise. But it is wholly in keeping with the determinist and transcendental doctrines of Islam. The characters submit to their environment; they are not moulded by it. Their qualities of mind and spirit are inherent, not acquired. They emerge victorious from their ordeals; except physically, they are not essentially changed by them. It is certainly questionable whether this, or our modern tendency to suppose that character is the changing product of environment, represents the truer view of human nature. It is worth recalling in this connection, that as late an English novelist as Charles Dickens also took a somewhat static view of character.

The style of the book is simple and direct. It retains the expressive idiom of colloquial Hausa, but it has clearly also been much influenced by the author's familiarity with the English novel form. His is not the allusive and meandering style of the Hausa fable, which, though suited to its purpose, is discursive and undisciplined.

1 Page 49 f.
2 Page 73

It has directness and economy arising from the fact that it has been schooled to a purpose not native to Hausa—the committing of a story to the written form, rather than the oral telling of a tale; the unfolding of a plot rather than the recounting of discrete incidents in a traditional sequence and pattern. The descriptions are not complex; nor is there any striving after literary effects. It is the direct almost photographic reproduction of what is seen by the eye, rather than what is imagined in the mind. But this stylistic economy achieves most satisfying prose description. Outstanding is the account of the sand-storm in the Sahara.[1] The initial undramatic picture of the travellers going about their various occupations during the noonday halt, is abruptly shattered by the appearance of the whirling black cloud on the horizon. The scene breaks up in panic as the cloud approaches. There is a moment in which the milling confusion and terror of the victims are vividly recorded; then silence and stillness descend once more. The effect of catastrophe is heightened by the way in which the sameness of the desert is restored, as if the sandstorm which has wiped out a whole caravan was simply a brief moment in the vastness of the Sahara. Equally vivid is the description of the child's kidnapping. The little boy's eager trustfulness is skilfully played off against the evil cunning of his kidnapper, and the scene in the cave is memorable for the way in which it portrays tension, the cold cruel threat of the knife, and the sheer physical terror of the child.[2]

The action of *Shaihu Umar* takes place at the end of the nineteenth century, and 1883, the date when the caravan left Kano for Ber Kufa was the year in which Sarkin Kano Abdullahi died and Bello succeeded. This was a troubled time in the history of the Hausa people. The Fulani conquests had taken place earlier in the century, and the old Habe chiefs had been overthrown. The initial reforms, and the strong government which the early Fulani emirs had introduced, had largely lapsed, for the later Fulani rulers,

1 Page 76
2 Page 42

though personally pious, often lacked both the militant zeal and the administrative ability of the founders. In consequence dynastic and tribal rivalries flared up in the course of the century following the conquest, and Hausaland remained in a state of constant insecurity and upheaval. In the south Sarkin Yaki Umaru Nagwamatse devastated Nupe, Zaria and Gwari country by his slave-raiding. He died in 1876, but was succeeded by his son Ibrahim Nagwamatse, an equally active slaver. At the same time the Gobirawa and the Habe of Nupe and Maradi constantly raided into Fulani territory. In the middle of the century the rebel Buhari was harrying Kano from Hadeja. At the end of the century Bornu and eastern Hausa were ravaged by Rabeh, while Kano was torn by constant revolt and factional struggle which culminated in the disastrous civil war between Alu and Tukur. In such unsettled conditions slave-raiding was rife, and the common people lived under the constant threat of enslavement. As Barth pointed out, slave-raiding involved not only the capturing of prisoners and the killing of full-grown men, but also the famine and distress which the raids left in their train.[1]

Although the Saharan trade in general had declined by the nineteenth century from the level which it had attained during its heyday of the fifteenth and sixteenth centuries, it was still important. As Boahen points out, it had become concentrated on four main routes which were Morocco–Taodeni–Timbuctu in the west; Ghadames–Air–Kano and Tripoli–Fezzan–Bornu in the centre, and Cyrenaica–Kufra–Waday in the east.[2] In the nineteenth century Kano was the most important centre for the trade in Hausaland and as Barth's account of the city makes clear, it was a busy and colourful metropolitan market which attracted all the peoples from the desert and from the countries to the south of it.[3]

1 *Travels*, iii, 225
2 'The Caravan Trade in the Nineteenth Century', *Journal of African History*, iii, 2, 1962, 349–359
3 Ibid. In fact, the decline of the Saharan caravan trade from its peak in the late Middle Ages has probably been over-stated. Our evidence suggests that despite the collapse of the Songhay empire, the trade across the Sahara continued to be substantial right up until the time of the European occupations and the building of railways.

12

In the Sahara itself the old security of the trade routes which had existed during the late Middle Ages had diminished with the overthrow of the Songhay empire. In place of the Askias, Timbuctu in the nineteenth century was ruled by weak and corrupt mulatto pashas, the descendants of the Arma, who were incapable of controlling the Touareg and other desert raiders preying on the caravans. It was such raiders as these that the Arabs were preparing to fight off when they were about to enter the Sahara, and Umar's fears when he saw them preparing their weapons were well-founded.

The route taken by Abdulkarim and Umar on their first journey appears to have been the easterly one from Kano to Birnin Kuka, and then through Darfur and northward, probably from El-Fasher, to the upper Nile. That taken by Umar's mother and followed again disastrously by Umar and Abdulkarim on their last journey was that from Kano to Birnin Kuka, and thence due north, leaving Lake Chad on the east, through Bilma, Yat, Gatron, Murzuk, and thus to Tripoli. On looking at the map we can see at once why the eastern route was impracticable during the time of the Mahdist rising in the Sudan, for it was in the whole area of Kordofan that the fighting took place.

The affair of Rabeh, which provides the final dramatic close to our story, was part of the general pattern of civil war and upheaval caused in the eastern Sudan by the activities of the slave-raiders. Rabeh was the lieutenant of the slaver Sulaiman Pasha, and when he was defeated Rabeh fled with the remnants of his army. He eventually reached Dikwa, in Bornu, where he set up his headquarters and from where he terrorised Bornu and eastern Hausa. He was killed in 1900 by the French, who by this time had begun their occupation of parts of the Sudan.

As for the trade in slaves, this also was already in decline by the time our story takes place. The efforts of the British consular agents in Tripoli and the Sahara had resulted in the traffic being considerably curtailed.[1] Indeed, as early as 1851 Barth had written 'the

1 A. Adu Boahen, *Britain, the Sahara and the Western Sudan 1788-1861*. Oxford, 1964, ch vii and passim

13

slave-trade at present is, in fact, abolished on the north coast'.[1] This was not entirely true, since slave caravans continued to cross the Sahara until the end of the century, and Boahen has stated that large caravans were still leaving Benghazi in 1905, bound for Wadai where they bartered guns for slaves.[2] Nevertheless, the scale of the trade had diminished by the end of the century. But the lot of those who were unfortunate enough to be enslaved had not improved, and Umar does not exaggerate when he states that twenty-five out of a total of eighty had died on the desert crossing.[3] Denham and Clapperton saw ample evidence of the numbers who succumbed on this terrible journey.

'During the last two days we had passed on an average from sixty to eighty or ninety skeletons each day; but the numbers that lay about the wells at El-Hammar were countless.'[4]

To the great hardship involved in trudging on foot through the sand the same witnesses testify.

'Some little girls and children of the Kafila, panting with thirst, augmented by fever and illness, were scarcely able to creep along the deep sand: the whips shaken over the head urged them on—for in justice it must be said, the Arabs use it but rarely in any other way—and not to urge them on would be still more cruel, for the resolution and courage of these poor things would never carry them through.'[5]

Monteil, whose work was published in 1895, has left us an account of the caravans which were still plying between Kano and the Saharan centres at the very end of the century, and of the Arabs who were established in the big northern termini of the trade routes.

'Each year towards the end of September there sets out from Air or Asben (a mountainous region of the central Sahara) a caravan

1 Op. cit., III, 135
2 Loc. cit.
3 Page 61
4 Denham and Clapperton, *Travels*, London, 1831, i, 144
5 Ibid. iii, 139

14

of three or four thousand camels called an *airi*. This caravan, loaded with cereals and dates, arrives at Bilma (south of the oasis of Kawar, to the north of Chad) there to exchange its cargo for the famous salt which is collected there. The airi, loaded with salt, returns to Tintelloust and then makes for Zinder and Kano.

'From Zinder part of the caravan goes to Katsina and Sokoto.

'The caravan arrives in Kano about January and there takes on the goods of the Arab merchants in order to transport them to Ghadames. These consist of ostrich plumes, a little ivory, and undressed skins. . . .

'Four or five hundred Arabs, representing the houses of Ghadames and Tripoli, have the monopoly of the trans-Saharan commerce; but this activity is, in my opinion, only a fifth of the total commercial activity of Kano which, therefore, is for the most part in the hands of the Hausa.'[1]

Such then was the background to the activities of men such as Abdulkarim, Ado and Ahmad.

Shaihu Umar is a tale of the *fin de siècle*—the last days of a century of turbulence, bloodshed, and slavery. From its turmoil Shaihu Umar himself at last finds sanctuary in his scholarly and pious vocation. The year 1900, in which he reached Rauta, was memorable in the history of the Hausa people. It ushered in a century of change unimagined by the men of his day. But here his story ends. We hope that others with the same gifts of understanding and of weaving a tale, will follow Shaihu Umar, and record for us the stories of their people in the years that followed.

MERVYN HISKETT

1 P.-L. Monteil, *De Saint-Louis a Tripoli par le lac Tchad*, Paris, 1895, 290–291

SHAIHU UMAR

by ALHAJI SIR ABUBAKAR TAFAWA BALEWA

translated by Mervyn Hiskett

Chapter One

God is the king who is greater than all other kings in glory, He is the most holy of all things, He is the king unto whom there is none like. Near the walled city of Bauci there is a little town called Rauta. In this little town there was once a certain malam, learned in the stars, in the Koran, and in the scriptures, and an upholder of the Faith. This malam was one of the men of this world to whom God has given the gift of knowledge. His name was Shaihu Umar. So great were his learning and wisdom that news of him reached countries far distant from where he lived. Men would come from other countries, travelling to him in order to seek knowledge. Before long the people coming to him foregathered, and became so numerous that they had no place to set up their compounds, so it became necessary for some of them to seek compounds in the little villages near to Rauta.

None who had studied under Shaihu Umar had ever known him impatient, nor had they ever known a day when they had come to study, and he had said that he was tired, except perhaps if he were unwell. And even if ill-health afflicted him, if it were not severe, he would without fail come out to teach. This Shaihu Umar was a man beyond all others, the like of whom is not likely to be found again. Whatever evil thing befell him, he would say, 'It is God who relieves all our troubles.' He never became angry, his face was always gentle, he never interfered in what did not concern him, and he never wrangled with anyone, let alone did he ever show even the slightest cantankerousness. Why, because of this character of his, it came about that in the whole country no-one ever criticised him, and many people began to say, 'Certainly this is no mere man, he is a saint.'

One day, just before evening prayer,[1] after Shaihu Umar had been teaching his students, they were all sitting discussing the affairs of the world, when one student asked him 'Master, I would like to ask you a little question, but I hesitate in case you should think that it is disrespect towards you that makes me ask'. Shaihu Umar answered him, 'Why, knowledge is never made complete except by asking, and what is more, no man knows everything. So ask me whatever you need to know, and have no fear in your mind. As for me, may God grant that I know what you ask me.'

The questioner said, 'May God grant you his forgiveness Malam, the things I want to know from you are two. First, that you should tell me from whence you come, and that you should tell me about your country. Are all the people of your country as you are? For, as for me, you certainly amaze me. And not only me; whoever knows you will be amazed at you. Secondly, I want you to tell me your origin, for I see that you are not like the people of our country. You have learning and speech like that of the Arabs, yet I see that you do not give yourself airs as they do.'

Umar answered him, 'Certainly you have asked me very sensible questions, to which I can, without doubt, give you the answers. But you have asked for a long story, and one which will cause wonder and pity in all who hear it. Now I will try to tell you about my country and my origin, and about my wanderings, and the difficulties I endured before I arrived here in your town.'

I AM A NATIVE OF KAGARA

Away back (began Shaihu Umar) I was a native of this country, but even so, I did not grow up and pass my boyhood here. It was far away in the country of the Arabs that I grew up. Long long ago I was a native of a certain country near Bida, and the name of our town was Kagara. My father was a tall light-skinned man whose

1 The Muslim prays five times in twenty-four hours; just before sunrise; at midday; in the late afternoon; at sundown; and during the hours of darkness.

craft was leather-working. My mother was a native of Fatika. Now when my mother was carrying me, my father died and left me an inheritance of six cows, three sheep, and his riding mare. At this time the mare was in foal. All these things were handed over to my mother, who was told to keep them until in God's good time she should give birth, for they were the property of her son, since this husband of hers had no other relatives to claim the inheritance.

So things went on until one day I was born, and I turned out to be a boy. Now when the naming day came round, my mother had one of my rams caught and slaughtered, and the name of 'Umar' was whispered in my ear.[1] Time passed until, when I was two years old (that is, the time for weaning), my grandmother on my father's side took me to wean me.[2] I lived with her until the time came when my mother wanted to marry again.

Then my mother said to my grandmother, 'You know that apart from you, I have no relations in this town besides this boy, and now I want to marry. What is more, many suitors have come forward to press their suit, saying that I must marry the one that I like best. I have come to you for advice. So-and-so and so-and-so seek my hand, but up to now I have not made up my mind which one I like best. I want first to hear what you have to say. Among them is a certain courtier, especially close to the Chief, called Makau.'

When my grandmother heard the name of Makau among the

---

1 'When the seventh day comes round, the naming-day, the husband's father kills a ram. The husband's mother brings out a new cloth which she gives to the child's mother, then she ties the baby on the midwife's back and they take him to have his head shaved. In the early morning they give him his name in the entrance-hut, only the malams and the men of the family are there. After this the husband's kinsmen distribute three calabashes of kolanuts if the child is a boy, two if it is a girl.' *Baba of Karo*, 140. The malam who performs the ceremony whispers the name, which is of course the child's Muslim name, into his ear. He customarily receives a reward for his services:
'At the naming ceremony and the funeral assembly
Their zeal is all for a little grain and dough.'
'The "*Song of Bagauda*": A Hausa king list and homily in verse—II', BSOAS, xxviii, 1, 1965, 132
2 A Hausa child is weaned two years after birth. It is customary for the grandmother to take charge of him during the weaning period. *Baba*, 145.

suitors, she said, 'My daughter, indeed God has brought you great good fortune![1] When there is one with good eyesight, would you marry a blind man? If you ask my advice, you should marry none save Makau. I know that he is a modest man, who is in no way mean-minded, and certainly if you marry him your home will be a happy one.'

My mother accepted this advice. The next day the marriage ceremony was performed, and a day was appointed upon which she was to move into her husband's compound.[2] When the time came my mother went to live in her own hut, and I remained with my grandmother. I lived happily with my grandmother, and then one day a fatal illness came upon her. When she realised that she was not to recover, she sent for my mother to warn her, saying: 'See now, I do not think that I shall rise again from this illness, so I want you to take this boy home with you, because I do not want to see him cry even a single tear. It would make me very unhappy to see that.' My mother replied, 'Very well.'

Shortly after we had left, my grandmother died. Many people assembled, prayers were said over her, and she was laid in her grave.

When this was all over, I was living comfortably with my mother in Makau's compound, when one day the Chief had all his courtiers summoned. When they had assembled he said to them, 'The reason I have summoned you is this. I want you to make ready, and set out on a raid on my behalf to Gwari country.[3] I am in dire need, and therefore I want you to make haste to set out, in the hope that you will return quickly.'

When the courtiers heard what the Chief had to say, they all went mad with joy. They were delighted, saying, 'Just give us half a chance, and we'll be off!' The reason for their delight was because,

1 Literally, 'God has given you a long ground-nut.'
2 After the marriage ceremony the Hausa bride waits seven days in her parent's compound before moving to her husband's compound. On the day that she joins him a feast is given. *Baba*, 113.
3 Birnin Gwari, to the west of Zaria. Gwari country was one of the main slave-hunting areas of Umaru Nagwamatse and his successors.

as you know, on a raid they would gain many cattle, and slaves as well. And then when they returned, the Chief would give them a part of everything which they had won. Thus if a man were to capture three slaves, the Chief would take two of them, and he would be allowed to keep one.

The reason for this raid that the Chief was planning, was that he wanted to obtain some slaves. Some he would put with his own, and send to Kano[1] so that clothes and saddlery might be bought and sent back to him, while others he would send to Bida[2] in order to procure muskets.

Among the horsemen whom the Chief had appointed as raiders was Makau. When the time came for their departure, after the Chief had sought an auspicious hour from a certain malam,[3] Makau came into his compound and gathered his family together. He said to them, 'Now you know that I am going on a raid to Gwari country, and I do not know when I shall return. Whether I shall be killed there, God knows best. For this reason I want to bid you all farewell, and I want you to forgive me for all that I have done to you, for any man in this world, if you live with him, some day you are bound to cause him unhappiness.'

His family all spoke up together. 'By God, you have never done anything to make us unhappy. We wish you a safe journey, and a safe return.' Thereupon all of us burst out crying, so that none of us could hear the other!

1 Kano was one of the main centres of the trans-Saharan trade during the nineteenth century, as Barth makes clear in his famous description of the city and its market.
2 The main town of Nupe province. Nupe was famous for its muskets, and the trade in muskets in exchange for slaves began during the reign of Sarkin Kano Kumbari (1731–1743), and Sarkin Nupe Jibrila. Palmer, *Sudanese Memoirs*, vol. iii, Lagos, 1928, 124.
3 One of the functions of a malam is to cast horoscopes and foretell auspicious times for undertaking journeys and other enterprises. This is done by the stars, and by other auguries. The practice is widespread throughout Hausa Islam, and indeed North Africa, although it is condemned by the orthodox.

'They practise divination that they may discern the hidden mysteries of God
In their drawings on the ground, because of their apostasy.
Both the fortune-teller and he who believes him,
The Angel of Hell-fire will they meet with!'

'The Song of Bagauda, II', 112

The raiders all began to make ready, and in the early dawn they set out and made for the interior of Gwari country. They continued until they reached a small pagan village on a rocky stronghold in the forest. On their arrival in this place, they all dismounted from their horses, and lay down at the foot of some thick shady trees, where no-one could see them. At this season the rains had begun to set in, and all the farmers were about to clear their farms. Now there was no way that these pagans could sow a crop sufficient to feed them for a whole year, so they had to come out of their towns and come down to the low ground to lay out their farms in the plain. Despite this however, they were not able to tend their farms properly, for fear of raiders.

When the raiders reached the village they hid on the edge of the farms. Early in the morning, just before the time of prayer, the pagans began to come out from their villages, making for their farms. The raiders crouched silently, watching everything that they were doing. They held back until all the people had come out. Then, after they had settled down to work, thinking that nothing would happen to them, the raiders fell upon them all at once, and seized men and women, and even small children. Before the pagans had realised what was happening, the raiders had already done the damage. At once other pagans began to sally forth, preparing to fight to wrest back their brothers who had been captured. Af! Before they were ready, the raiders were far away. They started to follow them, but they had no chance of catching them. Those in front got clean away, leaving their pursuers far behind.

SOMEONE SOWS DISCORD BETWEEN THE CHIEF AND MAKAU

When the raiders saw that they had escaped, they took to the high road, for, as you know, they would not have followed the high road in the first place, lest the pagans should catch up with them. Then, when they got onto the high road they made haste, each saying to his companion, 'Come on, come on'. They kept on going until, by

God's grace, they reached home safely. When they entered the town, each one made straight for the palace, bringing with him his booty from the raid. All of them had at least two slaves, and there were some with three slaves, and even some with four. Each of them presented before the Chief that which he had obtained. Except for Makau. On his return, he had not gone by way of the palace, but had gone straight to his own compound. But this was not with any deceitful intent.

When everybody was present, each one handed over what he had brought. Then the Chief said, 'Where is Makau? Was he perhaps killed out there, and you are hiding it from me?'

The whole company answered together, 'Oh no, God save your Majesty, but you know what men are like. As for us, we kept quiet right from the start, when we saw he was your favourite, so as to see how it would all turn out between you. For we well know that anyone who is trusted, and betrays the trust, God will punish him, let alone in a case such as that of you and Makau, to whom you have entrusted everything that you possessed. Let us now skin the monkey for you, right down to its tail! In this whole town you will never find one who betrays your trust like this Makau. Why, it's Makau who shames you by revealing all your secrets to the common people, who you see, are giving themselves airs now. Why, there is never a secret that you tell him that some of them don't hear about. You know, from the time that we set out on this raid until we returned, this fellow never ceased to abuse you, to such an extent that Sarkin Zagi[1] became angry and drew his sword, intending to strike off his head, until the Barde[2] had to bid him hold his hand. The reason that you do not see him here now is that he has gone by way of his own compound, in order to hide some of the slaves which he has acquired, for he captured four, two young girls, and two boys, but one of them is almost grown up. But of course, we don't know, let's just wait and see what he is going to bring.'

1 A functionary of the court, who runs in front of the chief's horse.
2 A mounted attendant of the chief.

When the Chief heard their words he said, 'So that's it, Makau has done well!'

After a little while Makau approached with the two young slaves whom he had captured, entirely unaware of what his fellow courtiers were plotting against him. Now these two slaves which he had brought were all that he had ever obtained, and the story that he had captured four slaves was a fabrication of his enemies. As Makau approached the gate of the palace, he saw from a distance the Chief seated outside, holding court. When the courtiers saw him they began to say, 'Aha, there's Makau coming with only two slaves, so he's hidden the other two, has he?' When Makau reached the Chief he prostrated himself in greeting, but the Chief did not reply. In the whole company there was not one who said as much as a single word to him. Each one just kept staring at him, and his rivals were overjoyed, as though they had been given hump to roast![1]

After a little while the Chief said, 'Makau, is it only now that you have arrived?' He replied, 'No, God save your Majesty, I went by way of my compound, so as to tether my horse and change my clothes, before coming to your presence.'

The Chief said, 'I see, and how many slaves did you get?'

Makau said, 'Two.'

The Chief said, 'Right. Are you sure you only got two? Do you agree that if I investigate and find that it was not two that you got, I should do to you whatever I like?'

Makau said, 'Most certainly, I agree.'

When they had finished this exchange, the Chief called the Sarkin Zagi and asked him, 'How many slaves is it that Makau brought back from the raid?'

Now all along the Sarkin Zagi had been waiting eagerly for this to happen, and he said, 'Four slaves, but he only entered the city

1 The hump of the humped cattle of Nigeria is considered a delicacy by the Hausa. Those who were given the task of roasting hump would expect to be given some for their trouble.

with two, because he sold the other two on the road to a caravan of Kano people who were going to fetch locust-bean[1] cake from Bauci.'

The Chief said, 'So, do you hear that Makau?'

Makau replied, 'God save your Majesty, I have nothing more to say, for these people have already told so many lies that there is nothing more that I can tell you that you will believe.'

MAKAU'S COMPOUND IS RANSACKED

Then the Chief became enraged, and sent the courtiers off and gave them permission to go and ransack Makau's compound, ordering them not to leave him a single thing, even if only a sleeping mat. The courtiers went and stripped his compound to the ground, even the grass with which the roofs of the huts were thatched, all was stripped. He had some cattle in a little village near the town, and there and then someone was sent to fetch them. Now when they went to bring back these cattle of Makau's, they included mine, which my father had left me as an inheritance, and also my sheep, and my mare, and her foal. After they had completely finished this pillage they gathered up the property and took it to the Chief.

When it was brought Makau rose and said to the Chief, 'God save your Majesty, I beg you, among this property there are some things which do not belong to me, such as this mare and her foal, the sheep, and some cattle. These things belong to a certain boy, an orphan, whose mother I married. I beg you, take out this orphan's property and restore it to him.'

On hearing this the courtiers all spoke at once, 'Aha, you hear, there he goes with those lies of his again! How do you come to be

1 The pod of the locust-bean (*parkia filicoidea*) contains a pulp which is scraped out to make flour. With this flour cakes are made which are used as one of the ingredients of soup.

> 'The grave-diggers should be given money and threshed corn
> On account of their work being arduous,
> (But) there shall be no reward from God; they have already had their pay;
> They have bought locust-bean cake and soup to mix it with.'

'*Bagauda*, II', 129.

making out that you've got an orphan's property in your keeping? May God save your Majesty, he's lying. This property of the orphan that he's talking about, it's not in his keeping at all, it's in the keeping of the boy's mother and she knows what she has done with it.' (At this time I was a small boy, hardly able to talk properly, much less could I understand what was happening. When they ransacked the compound, all I knew was that my parents were weeping.)

Then and there, without making any inquiries at all, the Chief accepted what the courtiers told him. After it was finished, he said to Makau, 'So, you see, this is the reward which you get from God for having betrayed my trust, after I had trusted you. Now I have nothing more to say to you; what has been done to you is sufficient. After this, as long as I am Chief in this town, I will not permit you to remain in it. And so I shall banish you to somewhere far away, not under my jurisdiction. However, I will not forbid you to take your family with you. Any one of your wives, if she loves you, let her follow you, and you can go together. But if she does not love you, then you must leave her behind.'

Makau said, 'God save your Majesty. I hear and I obey. But I beg you, in the majesty of your kingship, allow me a few days here to obtain certain provisions to eat on the road, for as you know, I am now going to an unfamiliar place.'

The Chief raised his head for a time. Then he answered Makau, saying that he agreed, but that he would give him four days only, to make ready for his exile.

Makau thanked him, got up, came back to his compound, and gathered all his family together, old and young, male and female, and said to us, 'Well now, you have seen how God has decreed that this thing should happen to me. The Chief has said that I must leave his country, but he will allow me to take with me any wife who wishes to follow me, and in addition he has said that I must leave this town within four days. Now what I want to say is this, if any woman among you is sure in her heart that she can bear to follow me, well and good, let her come.'

His whole family burst into tears together, saying, 'By God, we swear that even if it be no other country on earth that you are bound for, even if it be the next world, if it is possible to accompany you there, we shall accompany you.'

Makau asked us thrice, according to the Law, but not one of us changed his mind.

MAKAU IS BANISHED FROM THE TOWN

After this business with his family, Makau went out to the entrance hut of his compound and sat down, thinking about the country to which he should go, and then many people, his friends and others of their class, began to come to him, condoling with him in this unhappiness. I could see that most of the people, as they came, were weeping, and some of them would also come with a few cowrie shells[1] which they handed over to him, saying, 'Here's a little something in case you need to buy a drop of water to drink on the way.'

When it was time for evening prayer, Makau got up, performed his ablutions, and then said his prayers. This day it was my mother's turn to cook the supper.[2] After everybody had finished chatting, Makau went into his compound in order to lie down and sleep. When he came in he passed by my mother's hut, and found her weeping most bitterly. When he saw this he said to her, 'This is no matter for weeping, it has gone beyond tears. And even if it were not thus, since you are a Muslim woman, you ought to bear in mind that all things which befall a person come from God. So the best thing for us all is to trust God, who orders everything as he sees fit.'

My mother replied, 'Very well Makau, yet what in this world is to prevent me from weeping? You see, throughout the whole length

1 During the eighteenth and nineteenth centuries, and during the early years of the twentieth century, cowrie shells were the local medium of exchange throughout the Western Sudan, extending as far eastward as the western boundary of Bornu, and to Timbuctu in the north.
2 In a polygamous Muslim Hausa household the husband spends two nights with each wife in turn. It is the duty of the wife in question to prepare the supper on these occasions.

and breadth of this town I have no kinsfolk on my mother's side, let alone on my father's, and what's more, apart from this young orphan, I have no one, save you to whom God has joined me. And then I keep thinking about this evil thing that has happened to you, for it's certain that in this world, whatever affects your life, affects mine too. But my main concern is this young boy—I don't know what to do with him. Over and above all this, I had wanted to ask you, when you came back from the raid, for permission to go to my family's town in order to see my parents,[1] and then return here to you. And now, look what has happened.'

When Makau heard what she had to say he fell silent, thinking. After a little while he answered her, 'Truly you have many sorrows to bear, but even so, God will lighten all our troubles. Wipe away your tears, for all this is nothing in the plans of God. But as for what you say about going to see your parents, I will give you a little bit of advice. Now since things have turned out like this, and we are in this position, and I don't know for certain what town I shall settle in, I agree that you should go and visit your home; when I have found a place to settle down properly, I will send for you to come and join me there. As for the boy, whom you cannot very well take with you, the best thing is for you to leave him here with some reliable person until you come back from your journey and can take him over again.'

My mother replied, 'Very well.'

So it went on, until the promised four days' grace which the Chief had given Makau had expired. Early in the morning the Chief sent to tell him that on this day the promised time was up, and that he should make ready and await his messenger who would come and escort him out over the borders of the country. Even before it was morning Makau was already fully prepared, but the Chief's messenger did not set out to come to him until after morning

1 Even when a Hausa woman marries, her attachment to her own kinsfolk remains strong, and she will visit them from time to time. This is made clear by numerous references in *Baba*.

29

prayer. Makau was sitting watching the road and saw, coming towards him in the distance, the Sarkin Zagi and somebody else known as the Sintili[1] approaching on their chargers. When they reached him they said not a word to him except, 'In the name of God.'

Makau stood up and then they asked him, 'In which direction do you wish us to banish you?'

He replied, 'In the direction of Zazzau.'[2]

They said, 'Go on, let us proceed.'

They put him in front, and they drove him on until they brought him to the border. Here they left him where he had never been since the day that he was born. They said to him, 'Now you must decide where you want to go. As for us, this is where the Chief ordered us to stop. Here we leave you, and whether you die, or whether raiders find you and capture you, is no concern of ours!'

Makau said, 'So be it; when you arrive home, convey my thanks to the Chief, and as for you, may God bring you safely out of the forest. Amen.'

MAKAU MEETS A HUNTER

When they left him, he sought out the foot of a big tree and sat down, thinking, and calling on God and His Prophet,[3] until his heart was eased. When he raised his head, he saw a hunter strolling towards him, carrying nothing but his quiver and his bow. It was late evening, and Makau was by now almost dying of thirst. On seeing him the hunter made towards him, and found him sitting with his head on his knees. When he reached him, he greeted him, and Makau raised his head and returned his greeting.

After they had exchanged greetings, the hunter said to Makau, 'Slave of God, where have you come from? Why have you come

1 A court functionary whose duty is to carry the metal vessel containing the water which the chief uses for his ceremonial ablution before prayer.
2 Zaria Province
3 The Prophet Mohammed

to this place at this time? Have you been on a raid, has the day gone badly for you, and have you scattered in the forest?'

Makau replied, 'Not at all. But before all else, what I want most of all is that you give me some water to drink, then when I am feeling better, maybe I can tell you the story of my coming to this place.'

The hunter gave Makau some water. After he had drunk he waited a little until he had fully recovered, and then he said to the hunter, 'Praise be to God, I thank you, may God recompense you with good for this help which you have given me. Listen now to the story of my coming here.'

When the hunter had heard the story, he was astonished, saying, 'In truth, as God decrees a thing, so will it happen. An honest man will never be disappointed.'

Makau said, 'What is the reason for these words of yours?'

The hunter replied, 'I know well that had God caused you to meet with any of my brothers, and not with me, then for sure you would long ago have become a slave. But you see, since it was because of your honesty that this evil thing befell you, it has turned out not too badly. May God now make it easier still, and may He assist us in all that we do, and cause us to prevail over our enemies. Now then, to what town do you intend to go?'

Makau said, 'Originally, I had thought of going to some little village between Zazzau and Kano, in order to settle there. But I also want this village where I settle to have good land for growing crops, for when I have found a good place to live, the craft which I intend to take up is farming. After I have settled in, and got my compound straightened out a little, I want to send for my family to come.'

YOU SHOULD SETTLE IN MAKARFI

The hunter said, 'Certainly in choosing a craft you have made an excellent choice. And so I will give you a little advice. If you accept it, good—if not, that's up to you. Beyond Zazzau there is a little town called Makarfi. The people there are well known for husbandry; farming there is profitable and what's more, crops are always bountiful. I think the best thing for you is to go there and settle. You see, there is nobody there who will interfere with you. Among the people of the town there is no-one who meddles in his fellow townsman's business, for all of them are reasonably well-off. You know, there is never much back-biting where there is plenty, but only where poverty has its roots.'

Makau lowered his head for a time, then he looked up, and said, 'Most certainly I shall follow your advice, for I see you have really taken a liking to me. But I also want to ask you if you have any other little secret which I can use to escape from the dangers which I shall meet before I reach Makarfi.'

The hunter took out a little leather amulet on a chain,[1] gave it to him, and said, 'I can help you with this, and I also wish you a safe journey. May God ward off ill-fortune.' They bade each other farewell and parted, each one of them weeping.

---

1 The use of such charms is very common among the Hausa, and indeed all the peoples of West Africa. 'The talismanic charms fabricated by Moslems, it is well known, are esteemed efficacious, according to the various powers they are supposed to possess; and here is a source of great emolument as the article is in public demand from the palace to the slave's hut; for every man (not by any means exempting the Moslems) wears them strung round the neck, either in cases of gold, silver or the hairy hide of wild beasts, such as lions, tygers, monkeys, elephants, sloths, etc. Some are accounted efficacious for the cure of gunshot wounds, others for the thrust or laceration of steel weapons, and the poisoned barbs of javelins or arrows. Some, on the other hand, are esteemed to possess the virtue of rendering the wearer invulnerable in the field of battle, and hence are worn as a preservation against the casualties of war,' Dupois, *Journal of residence in Ashantee*, London, 1824, Part II, xl.

Also Mungo Park, *Travels*, London, 1799, 38, '. . . these horns were highly valued, as being easily convertible into portable sheaths, or cases, for containing and keeping secure certain charms or amulets called *saphies*, which the Negroes constantly wear about them. These saphies are prayers, or rather sentences from the Koran, which the Mahomedan priests write on scraps of paper, and sell to the simple natives, who consider them to possess very extraordinary virtues. Some of the Negroes wear them to guard against the bite of snakes or alligators; and on this occasion the saphie is commonly inclosed in a snake or alligator's skin, and tied round the ancle. Others have recourse to them in time of war, to protect their persons against hostile weapons; but the common use to which these amulets are applied is to prevent or cure bodily diseases; to preserve from hunger and thirst, and generally to conciliate the favour of superior powers under all the circumstances and occurrences of life.'

32

After Makau had said farewell to the hunter, he arose and remained for a short while in the place where he stood, for he did not know which road to follow to take him towards Zazzau. When the hunter saw this he returned, took his hand and they walked on until they came upon a cattle track near to a little village.

When they came to the spot the hunter said to him, 'You see this little village in front of us, that's the way you should go, but do not allow yourself to go inside because, very probably, if you do go in, you will never come out again. The best thing to do is to skirt the edge of the village, and so pass it by. And when you are going to pass it, be careful not to go to the north of it, because to the north of the village there is the farm of a certain man who is a very power-ful sorcerer. Any man, whether he is a stranger or a slave fleeing back from some other country, when he reaches this farm, he will usually stop there, not knowing what road he should take, and inevitably he will go into the farm. Now this man never leaves his farm and thus, when he sees someone stop close by it, wandering around as if lost, he comes and captures him and enslaves him.'

Makau said, 'Right, I understand.' Once again they said goodbye. Makau went on his way, and the hunter turned back towards the place where he had first met Makau.

Makau took the road until he reached the place where the village was. When he got there, he avoided going inside, and he carried out all that the hunter had told him. From the time that he took to the road he did not even turn his head to look at the village until he was absolutely certain in his own mind that he had left it well be-hind him. When he saw that he had got safely away from the vil-lage, he made for the foot of a tree, sat down and rested, and ate a little food.

No sooner had he sat down than he heard the sound of horse's hooves to the right of him. He also heard men talking, each one telling his companion all about what he had done when they had been to certain places raiding. On hearing this, Makau climbed up the tree beneath which he was sitting, and hid in its branches.

When they reached the place one of them said, 'You know, at this place I once had words with so-and-so and so-and-so when we were coming back from a raid. On that day we had got nothing except one little boy who was no more than seven years old, and there were three of us.

'When we arrived here, we stopped to rest, and then one of us said, "Now then, what can we do with this boy? How can each of us get the reward for his trouble out of him?"

'On hearing these words, the one who had the boy immediately spoke up and said, "Hey you, what do you mean by this nasty talk? You're an ungrateful chicken![1] How can you say that you want some profit from this boy, after I had all the trouble, and I captured him all by myself. If it is all that easy, why didn't you capture one of your own?"

'The other, on hearing this, at once drew his sword, and said, "So that's it, is it! I'll show you that this boy is not yours alone."

'He raised his sword and without a moment's hesitation, he sliced off the boy's head. Then he said to his owner, "There, you said you captured him. Take the trunk as the reward for your trouble; as for the two of us, the head will be enough!"

'The other said, "Good enough!"'

After the men had finished chatting they rested, and then they got up, and each one sprang on to his horse. They took the high road in great haste. When Makau saw that they were well away, he climbed down. On his way down he saw something at the foot of the tree—why! it was a purse that one of the men had dropped, and it was full of silver dollars.[2] He picked it up and took to the road,

---

1 A reference to the Hausa proverb, 'Chicken, eat and wipe your beak' (without saying 'thank you').

2 The Spanish dollar and the Austrian Maria Theresa dollar were also used as coinage in the Western Sudan during the nineteenth century. Barth states that two thousand five hundred cowries equalled one silver dollar (*Travels*, ii, 144, and passim). Silver dollars are still to be found in Hausaland today, but are now normally used for ornaments, or in dowries.

following in their tracks for a day and a night without resting, let
alone stopping to eat food.

HE SEES THE RAMPARTS OF THE CITY

As he travelled on, he caught sight of the ramparts of a town away
in front of him to the right. By now the horsemen had already
entered the town. Makau continued on his way until he reached
the town gate, and entered. He said to the gate-keeper, 'Malam,
what town is this?'

The gate-keeper answered, 'This is the town of Zazzau, my
friend.'

On hearing this Makau heaved a sigh, and said, 'Praise be to God.
God is the bringer of success!'

There and then he made friends with the gate-keeper, so that the
gate-keeper said, 'It gladdens my heart to see you, you must be my
guest.'

Makau was delighted, and lodged at the gate-keeper's compound.
When it was night they had supper. After they had finished eating
and had washed their hands, they began to talk about the world.
Makau told the gate-keeper the whole story of all that had happened
to him.

The gate-keeper asked him, 'Where do you intend to go to now?'

Makau said, 'I have heard of a certain village in this country,
called Makarfi. I want to go there, to see whether I can settle there,
for I have heard that the land is good for farming.'

The gate-keeper said, 'Excellent, and I have a full brother over
there, his name is Tanimu. When you leave, I'll give you a letter
for him.'

When dawn broke, Makau went to the gate-keeper and said that
he was going to set out, but that he would like him to let him have
a boy, so that they could go to market, and he could buy certain
tools. The gate-keeper gave him his boy, and they set off. Makau
bought a weeding hoe, an axe, a harvesting tool, and a long-handled

35

hoe. When he had completed his purchases, he returned home. He said goodbye to the gate-keeper, who brought some food for the journey and gave it to him. Then he wrote a letter to his brother Tanimu and said,

'Greetings to you. I am sending this man called Makau to you. He is a good man. Ask him for his story, and the reason that made him leave his native town. He says that he wishes to find some place to settle, in order to farm. I would like you to set him up comfortably, and keep an eye on him. Give him a farm and a place where he can build a compound, for he has a family who are coming later on.'

When he had finished it, he gave it to him. Makau thanked him most earnestly, and they said goodbye. The gate-keeper called his boy to set him on the road. Makau started out and continued until he came to Makarfi. He asked for Tanimu's compound, and was shown it. Then he went there and gave him the letter. When Tanimu read it he welcomed him, lodged him in his compound, and brought him food. After Makau had finished eating, he told him his whole story.

Tanimu said, 'I see. Tomorrow, if God spares us, I will show you a farm. And there is also a compound where my mother died recently. If it suits you, you can do it up and live in it.'

HE SENDS FOR HIS FAMILY TO COME

Makau settled at Makarfi. He tilled his farm, repaired his compound, and bought two slaves with the money that he had found, so that he began to prosper, and to feel at home. Then he went to Tanimu and told him that he wanted to send for his family to come.

Tanimu said, 'Quite right, this is most important, for a respectable and worthy man such as you should not live without a family. Now I have a boy, from Kagara, called Isa. If you have no-one to send, then he can go.'

After two days had passed, Makau made ready for Isa's departure.

He bought a gown from Tanimu, an excellently embroidered one, of the type made in Zazzau, and he wrapped it in a scrap of cloth and gave it to Isa, telling him to present it to the Chief of Kagara. He also fetched some little mementoes of Zazzau, and said that they were to be given to certain of his friends there in Kagara. Finally he gave him two caps, one of which he was to give to Sarkin Zagi, and one to the Sintili. He brought a small quantity of cowrie shells and gave him, and told him to buy food for the women pending their arrival. Then he said to him, 'Among my wives there is a certain young girl, a native of Fatika. When I was about to leave she asked me permission to go and see her parents. Now then, if you arrive and find that she has gone, leave a message for her, to say that she should make haste and join me and her fellow wives here. And when she comes, let her bring her son, the orphan. That's all. May God bring you back safely.'

On the day that Isa arrived in Kagara, he did not rein in his horse until he arrived at the palace. He went and delivered Makau's present to the Chief, and told him Makau's wishes concerning his family.

The Chief said, 'Very well. Let him be taken to Makau's compound, and let him lodge there pending the time that Makau's family are ready, and then let them depart.'

Isa went and settled in. When it was time for evening prayer, he had the hats which Makau had sent them delivered to the Sarkin Zagi and the Sintili, and he gave the rest of the mementoes to the people to whom Makau had sent them, and they were delighted. After he had finished distributing these things, he went to Makau's family and told them why he had come to them. They were so happy that you would have taken them for those who had fallen into the waters of the river of Paradise![1]

Then Isa enquired, 'Where is the girl, the native of Fatika, or has she already left?'

1 *Alkausara*. This is the Arabic *al–Kawtharah*, the name given to the one-hundred-and-eighth chapter of the Koran, and which is said by the exegetists to be the name of one of the rivers of Paradise.

The wives said, 'No, no, there she is. She's been waiting all this time for a message from him.'

Isa said to her, 'Makau says you should go, but that you should hurry back and join him there. And when you set out, take your son with you.'

She replied, 'Very well. May God spare us, and grant us the good fortune to meet again.'

Makau's family spent four days packing up and then on the fifth day Isa went and took leave of the Chief, and the following day they set out. My mother and I were left in Kagara. After Makau's family had left, my mother made ready for the journey to Fatika. On the eve of her departure she handed me over to a certain Sokoto man, called Buhari, who had been on neighbourly terms with my own father.

As soon as it was light I saw my mother going to and fro among the compounds. On this day I do not think she had even a proper drink of water, for she did not sit down in one place, only busying herself going among the compounds of her friends[1] until night fell. When she had finished all this going to and fro, she returned to Buhari's compound and lay down, weeping all the time. As for me, at this time nothing worried me at all. I was perfectly happy, for in the compound I had found other children as playfellows.[2]

UMAR IS ADOPTED

After night had fallen and the town was silent, my mother got up and went to one of Buhari's wives, called Amina, in whose hut I was, and she said to her, 'Amina, I want to say goodbye to you now, for it is my intention to set out before the call to dawn prayer. Now

1 The Hausa word *kawa* means 'a girl's bond-friend', and implies a special relationship and mutual obligations between two age-mates. This is discussed on p. 33 of the Introduction to *Baba*, and Baba frequently refers to this institution when telling her story.
2 Literally 'children, my brothers'. In a Hausa polygamous family the task of mothering the children is shared to some extent among all the wives, and the children in turn regard each wife as 'mother'.

please be patient, you know what the boy is like; whatever he wants to do, if he's not allowed to do it, he'll cry, but if he is allowed to do everything that he wants to do, he'll suffer for it in the future. The best thing is for you always to keep a firm hand on him, and don't bother yourself with thinking, "This boy is not mine"; by God, you and I, we are one, since God has joined us together, and we have been living on terms of friendship.'[1]

Amina said, 'To be sure, all that you have said is right, and I hope that God will give me strength to bear my burden.' After this they sat chatting until we children in her hut had gone to sleep.

When they had been chatting for a time, sleep began to overcome them, and my mother got up and went to lie down; but not a wink of sleep did she get for her heavy thoughts about what might happen on the road before she reached home, and for her fears about leaving me in a town where I had no relatives on my mother's side, let alone my father's. She was still brooding over this when she heard the cock crow. She got up, took up her load, and started on her way. Alas, fate had already forestalled her. I was not to see her again until after many a long year!

SOMEONE KIDNAPS ME

Of all this that had happened, I heard nothing. It was not only that I knew nothing, for at this time I was only about four years old, and wouldn't have understood, even if I had heard. From the time that my mother left Kagara I didn't even notice any change as far as I was concerned. I was eating and drinking as usual, and there were other children with whom I played all the time. And this Amina, the wife of Buhari, with whom I was living, never lost her temper with me. Whatever I did was always right. If I did something really naughty, when she raised her hand to smack me, she would stay her hand and say, 'Good Lord, what a witless boy!' She didn't like me to be separated from her, even for a moment, she always

1 A reference to the *kawa* relationship.

liked us to be together. When I wandered off, she at once became anxious, and came out and went to the compounds of the other children with whom she knew I was playing, and brought me back.

One day a number of us were playing together at the door of our compound—there were about nine of us children. Then we saw a man dressed in a wide gown with a big pocket coming towards us. We all stopped playing and stared, watching him until he came to where we were.

When he reached us we greeted him, '*Sannu Baba.*'[1]

He said, 'Is the master of the house at home?'

One boy from among us, a little older than the rest, said, 'No, he went off into the country, but he'll be back tomorrow.'

The man stood still, watching us as we played; then after a while he asked us our names. Each of us told him his name. When he heard my name I saw him stop suddenly, and fix his eyes on me. Now of all the children there, I was the smallest. After a little he called me saying, 'Hello Umar, you know me, now don't you? Where is your mother, where's your father? Let's go and I'll take you to your father, eh?'

I said, 'Yes please.'

Immediately, I saw him put his hand into a little bag he had and take out some fried meat together with some cowrie shells, and he gave them to me. Now you know what a child is like: I just took them, skipping happily. He took my hand and we started off as if he was going to take me to where my mother and father were. As for me, I started to follow him, with my cowrie shells in my hand, chewing at the piece of meat. We went on, he holding my hand, until we came out of the town. When we got outside the town I felt him draw me towards him and he entered a shallow ditch. We continued walking until I became tired, and was on the point of crying. Then he lifted me up on his shoulders and gave me some more meat.

We continued like this with me on his shoulders, from about

1 'Hello, Papa.' *Sannu* is the universal Hausa greeting.

midday until just before evening. Now the rest of the children with whom I had been playing, when they didn't see me any more, they began to cry. Then the people in the compound heard and sent a slave girl to see what was the matter. When she came out and asked the children why they were crying, they told her that Umar had got lost, and they couldn't find him. They said also that when they had been playing during the day, they had seen some man with a big pocket come and take me away, saying that he was going to take me to my mother and father. When the slave girl heard this she cried out in God's name and went into the compound to the rest of the family, to tell them what had happened.

When Amina heard, she burst into tears, saying, 'This is too dreadful to bear, Umar must have been carried off by some kidnapper. Whatever am I going to do with myself? When his mother returns and doesn't find him, what shall I say?' Then she threw herself down and began to roll on the ground, weeping and wailing until the whole town heard her. There and then they began to beat the drums and before night prayer was called every single one of the men in the town was out in the country looking for me.

But I and the man who had stolen me knew nothing of what was going on. When he saw that it was night, he took me down from his shoulders and sat me in a little cave in the rock, then he himself entered. He took out meat and some sweetmeat from his bag, and gave me, and he fetched water and gave me some to drink. We sat there in the cave, and now I was not worried about anything, because my tummy was full! As for him, he intended that I should rest a little, and that we should then go on.

I was sitting there and he was eating, when I saw him draw back his hand from the food, and stop chewing what was in his mouth. He stood quite still, like a horse when it hears something move. He remained a long time like this, and then he got up stealthily, knelt down on his knees and peeped outside. In a little while I began to hear the voices of people to the north of us. Immediately he heard this, I saw him put his hand in his bag and take out a little leather amulet with which he struck me on the head.[1] Then he untied a knife from the cord hanging round his neck and said to me, 'You know, these men have come out walking in the forest to catch children and eat them. It may be that you'll see someone you know among them, but do not let yourself answer, even though he calls your name, for if you answer you can be sure I'll cut your throat with this knife.' Then he unsheathed it and showed it to me. When I saw it flashing in the white light of the moon, my whole body began to shiver, and I soiled my pants.

When the people who were looking for me came near to the cave where we were, one of them said, 'Don't let us pass this place, because I used to know that somewhere around here there was a cave where once, when we came out to hunt him, we caught a kidnapper who had stolen a girl. Just let's go and look there first, and if there's nothing there, we'll go on.' We could hear all that they said. Then the man took his knife and put it to my throat, and said that if I said a word, or made the slightest movement, he would surely kill me.

THEY SEEK ME AND DON'T FIND ME

The people came on, chatting with each other, until they reached the mouth of the cave where we were. When they arrived one of them called out my name, 'Umaru, son of Makau' (for this was the name by which Amina was calling me). He went on calling, and I could hear him, but I was not able to answer, for fear of the sharp blade. They continued to call until they were tired. No-one answered them, and not one of them peeped into the cave, let alone entered. Then they returned home. The rest of the people meanwhile, had ransacked the forest, but not a sign of me had they seen. When they were tired, they too turned for home. As they went they said to each other that when this boy's mother heard about it, she would surely go mad or die.

1 See page 32, note 1. This was no doubt a charm to procure invisibility.

When the people reached home, they told Amina that they had not found me. She burst out weeping, and they all stood round her, bidding her be patient, for this was God's will. She dried her tears and went into her hut. But when she saw the wooden bowl of *tuwo*[1] which she had laid out for me, and the place where I used to sleep, the whole world became black with sorrow for her, and she fell upon the bed, and began to weep, all alone. From the day that I was lost, she never regained her peace of mind until she joined my mother at Fatika.

A HYENA DEVOURS MY KIDNAPPER

Those who were seeking me returned home at midnight. When the man who had kidnapped me heard that the forest was silent, he said to me, 'Now we have rested, haven't we? Let's get up and go on.' Then he picked me up and put me astride his neck, and set off with me into the forest, until we reached a little farm hut. Now by the time we arrived here it was dawn, and he took me down from his neck, saying he was tired. Then we entered the farm hut so that he could have a nap. He pulled me in behind him, and we went in together and lay down, and in a little while sleep overcame him. I did not feel sleepy, for I had already slept when I was on his back. Now no sooner had he fallen asleep than he began to snore so loudly that it terrified me. He had originally put me behind him when he was about to lie down, but when he started this snoring fear gripped me, and I rose up and got into a basket which the owners of the farm had left in the hut, and there I remained.

I had not been there long before I began to hear the growling of some frightful thing behind the hut. It was the growling of a hyena which had come out hunting, and had still not found anything by the time dawn came. She was about to return to her cave when she heard the snoring of my master, and prowled round the

1 A food made from the flour of guinea-corn or bulrush millet. The staple food of Hausaland.

43

hut to see what it was. Now you know what a farm hut is like. There was no strong fence round it, nor even a grass mat to screen the door. When the hyena came to the door of the hut, she stopped, deliberating as to whether she should come in or retreat. It was almost daylight. She plucked up her courage, pushed in her head, and came in. She found the man by the door, and she stood over him, sniffing at where his breath came out. Then I saw her fix her teeth in his windpipe, and without the slightest pause, and with no difficulty whatsoever she severed his head from his body, like a man taking a pair of scissors and snipping off a tender shoot.

Throughout all that the hyena was doing, the man did not awake. You know how death is; any living thing, when it is at the point of death, it suffers a last agony. So, when the wind briefly touched this man where the head had been severed, I saw him begin to kick,[1] and the hyena pause. When he had quite finished kicking, and she was sure that all life had left him, she snatched up the trunk, slung it over her back, and made for her cave, leaving the head in the hut with me.

Dawn broke, the sun came out, and I got up and went outside. I went to the foot of a locust bean tree on the farm, and sat down, playing with some pebbles. When the sun was well up, and I began to feel hungry, I started to cry, calling out 'Papa, papa'. No-one answered me. After I had been crying for a long time, I saw some people coming in the distance. It was the owners of the farm. I began to cry even more, and did not stop until they reached me. When they arrived they saw that I was a very small boy. They asked me what had happened to me, and I told them something like this, for at this time I didn't really know how to tell anybody anything. I said, 'Yesterday hyena eat papa bye-byes, papa head inside.' After I had said this one of the women said, 'Ayya, he

---

1 This reference to the wind arises from the fact that the Hausa have observed the 'reaction time' between the inflicting of a wound and the sensation of pain and the accompanying reflex. This they explain by saying that the pain is not felt until the wind touches the wound.

means to say that yesterday in the night a hyena devoured his father and left his head inside the hut.'

The rest said, 'That must be right; you, boy, where's your father?' Then I pointed to the hut where I had slept. There and then they went there, and as soon as they came to the door they began to see blood spattered on the wall, as if a cow had been slaughtered.

THE HUSBAND COMES

While this was going on, the husband of these women whom I was with, arrived and found us standing at the door of the hut, the women exclaiming and calling on God and His Prophet in the way that women do. On his arrival they told him all that had happened; he too called on God and His Prophet, picked up the head that the hyena had left, went to the edge of the farm, and buried it. After this, he looked at the man's clothes and began to search through what was in them. On unfolding the dead man's gown, he came on a large satchel containing nothing but fried meat, some sweets, baked flour, and a small calabash. He inspected the under-shirt and found two amulets, one covered with skin from a leopard's forehead, with a chain attached to its tag. The other one covered with the skin of the electric catfish, and sewn with monkey sinews. This second amulet moreover, had been wrapped in a scrap of *saki*[1] cloth, in which had also been placed a piece of human fat, with which he had greased the amulet. To this had been added the eye of a baby.[2]

To cut a long story short, when he looked carefully at the property of the dead man, he sighed deeply and said, 'Certainly this man was not the boy's father. There is no doubt he had stolen him from somewhere, for the only people who go in for trappings of this kind are kidnappers or highway robbers.'

1 A locally woven cotton material with black and white check pattern.
2 See page 32, note 1

After he had said this, he turned to me and asked me some questions which I can no longer remember. He spoke in vain. I did not even pay attention to what he was saying, let alone understand it. I was just playing on the ground together with his little children.

ONCE AGAIN I AM GIVEN FOR ADOPTION

When he saw that I paid no attention to him, he said to one of his wives, 'So-and-so, it is you who have no son. Very well, here you are, God has given you one. Look after him, and may God grant you joy in him.' She knelt and thanked him. Then she picked me up and asked me my name. I told her and she was happy.

After this, they got down to their farmwork. They worked on and on, while we went on playing until it was noon. Then they went to a stream and washed themselves. After they had finished, they returned to the locust bean tree where we were, and sat down to take a drink of water before going home. Then I saw one of them uncover a large calabash. She took out some lumps of locust-bean flour,[1] mixed them with flour, added water, and gave each one a portion. We little children were given ours in a ladle, scraping it out with our fingers.

After we had finished drinking the locust bean gruel, each woman took up her child and slung it on her back.[2] And as for me, my mother picked me up, put me on her back, and we set out for home. The head of our family was behind with a quiver and bow slung across his shoulders, and his two younger brothers were in front with their weapons slung. We children and women were in between.

We had hardly left the farm when we heard the distant hoof beats of horses in the forest, and people calling out, 'To horse, to horse, today your beds will lie empty!'

Not one of us took any notice of what they were saying, but just

1 See page 26, note 1
2 Hausa women carry their babies in a shawl wound round the breast and upper back. This holds the child firmly against the mother's back.

kept on going. But although no-one showed any sign of taking notice, each one's heart was quaking, and there was not one whose blood did not turn to water.[1] Each of us just kept walking in a daze. We continued to hear horses galloping and men talking, but saw no-one.

Then a little later we saw in the distance a horseman on a grey horse, clad in chain mail. He set his stallion at us, crying out, 'To-day your beds shall lie empty!'

On hearing this the head of our family said, 'God willing, it's your bed that will be the loser, because perchance today you will be left dead on the greensward!'

Immediately I saw him reach out his hand to his quiver, and take out an arrow, the whole shaft of which had been treated with poison. He fixed it on the bow string and knelt down, awaiting the horseman. As for the horseman, having set his horse at us he charged straight down on us without slackening speed. When the head of our family saw that he was near, he drew his bow, and loosed an arrow at him. Immediately the horseman interposed his shield, and before the head of our family had time to draw another arrow he had ridden him down, and left him flat on his back, dazed, as if his life had left him.

At this moment our presence of mind failed us. We simply stood and looked, staring at what had happened. Very soon afterwards we saw about seven horses making for us at the gallop. On seeing them each one of us ducked and took to his heels like a dog.[2] The other women fled and left my mother who was carrying me on her back. She was unable to run because she had slashed her foot with a harvesting tool.

THE HORSEMAN CAPTURES US

When the horseman who had ridden down the head of our family saw this, he dismounted from his horse and dragged my mother,

---

1 Literally, 'and there was not one who had any spine in his body'
2 Literally, 'borrowed a dog's stomach'

A Caravan Entering Kano City

A Hausa Town

A Hausa Village

Market at Sokoto

Return of the Sultan From an Expedition

Hausa Men on Horseback

A Slave Caravan

The Castle and Town of Tripoli in the 19th century

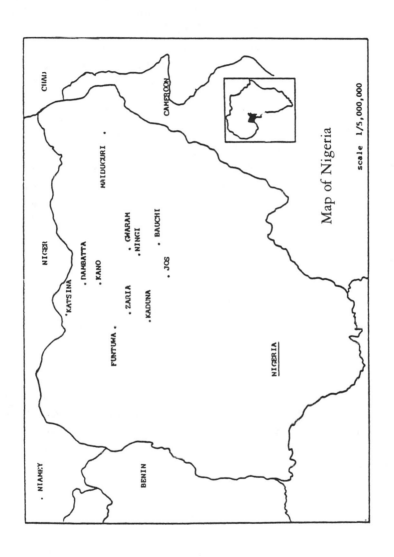

Map of Nigeria

scale 1/5,000,000

with me on her back, and bound us firmly to the head of our family with the leading rein of his horse. When the rest of the horsemen saw this they closed in behind our companions, and I do not know how it all ended for them. I think they captured them, because each one of them had a child on her back.

After the horseman had bound us with one hand behind the neck, he put us in front of his horse and drove us towards his town. We journeyed on until dawn. When the morning came he took me from my mother's back and put me on the pommel of his saddle, for he had pity on my mother who was carrying me. We travelled for about four days, and then found ourselves in Kano. Now this man was one of the head slaves of the Chief. He had become hard-up, and had taken a little trip in order to see what he could find to make ends meet. But when we got inside the city no-one would look at us because of the great anguish and unhappiness which we had endured.

MY MOTHER IS WITHOUT NEWS

Of all the things that had happened to me, my mother knew no-thing, for when she reached Fatika she found that her father had been arrested on a charge of witchcraft and taken to Zazzau. There she was, awaiting his return so that she might then come and take me with her to join Makau in Makarfi. After she had been two months and eleven days in the town, her father returned from the city, having been released and the charge dismissed. For when they had come before the court the Chief had severely rebuked the chief men of Fatika for the evil which they had done to him, and had said that there was no such thing as a sorcerer in this world. But he had not said this until my mother's father had promised to give him two milch cows. When he was about to leave Zazzau the Chief had sent with him a certain courtier to bring back the cows. He arrived with the courtier, who was given the Chief's cows. When they were given to him he said, 'A'a! Are you going to let me go off like this?' Thereupon, without further argument my mother's father brought a young she-goat and gave him, and he drove it off home. My mother's father was left with only a young heifer and one billy-goat with a coat so long that it touched the ground.

The people of the compound were delighted that the head of the house had returned safely. Large numbers of his friends came to congratulate him on his escape. After the visitors had all gone, my mother had found him in a hut, and congratulated him and wished him good fortune. When she went into the hut she had burst into tears. You know what women are like when they are happy! He had asked her for all her news, and she had told him everything, from beginning to end, without forgetting a single thing. Then he gave her his blessing, and said that she should persevere and do her best, and that after a few days she should return to Kagara and pick me up, and then go on to Makau.

She began to prepare for the journey. After she had finished her preparations, the day before she was due to set out, she went to her father and requested him to let one of the sons of the family escort her.

He said, 'Very well, go with Dabo.' Dabo was called, and was informed that he was to escort my mother to Kagara. After they had finished preparing, just before late afternoon prayer, she took a pitcher to draw water from a well which was close by the road used by traders going to Kagara. She had just lowered the bucket to draw water, when she saw far away in the distance, some women with their heads covered, and a rider coming from the direction of Kagara. She at once drew up her bucket and stood still, watching until they came near. When they approached, she saw that the rider was none other than Buhari. On looking at the faces of the women, she was sure she recognised Amina. At once she ran and embraced her, crying and bidding her welcome. She knocked over her pitcher, took Amina's bundle, and went ahead of her to where Buhari had dismounted. When she saw that they were all properly lodged, she returned home to prepare some food for them. At this time she had not noticed that I was not among the party.

She returned to the compound, informed her father of all that had happened, and asked to be given some good food which she could take to her guests. Right away two hens were caught and slaughtered, rice was taken from her mother's bin,[1] it was pounded, winnowed and washed, and made into fine *tuwo*.

As darkness fell, my mother took the food and went to the place where Amina and the rest were lodging. She put the food down and returned to her compound to eat her own food. After she had finished her meal, and was sure that they too had finished, she went back to them, to hear their news. On arriving she found Amina in a state of great distress, weeping and her eyes all swollen. When she saw her in this state, she went to one side, squatted down and put her head in her hands.

After a little Amina stopped crying and wiped her tears, and they exchanged greetings. Then my mother asked her why she was crying.

Amina replied, 'Nothing.'

My mother said, 'Please, if anything has happened, tell me; keeping it back doesn't make it any better.'[2]

My mother began to think in her heart that perhaps God had called me, after she had left Kagara. But Amina kept silent and said nothing.

This was how things were when Buhari came in to greet my mother. He came and found them sitting forlornly. He went in and sat down. My mother welcomed him and they greeted each other. She asked him for news of how things were in Kagara, and where he was intending to go. Well, you know what men are. Without more ado he spoke up and said to her, 'All are well in Kagara. Now I am intending to go to Hausa country to visit the tomb of a great saint, Shaihu Usumanu dan Fodiyo.[3] After this, I

---

1 In the polygamous family each wife has her own corn bin.
2 Literally 'leaving shit in the belly is no remedy for hunger.'
3 Usumanu ɗan Fodio ('Uthmān b. Fūdī), the Fulani revivalist preacher who, in 1804, led a successful holy war against the Habe chiefs. By 1810 he had conquered most of the Hausa states, and had replaced the Habe rulers with Fulani emirs, thus founding the Fulani dynasties. His tomb is situated near to Sokoto, and is a place of pilgrimage.

want to go and see certain maternal uncles of mine at Tureta, and from there I shall go on to Dingyadi to my mother, for it is a long time since we have seen each other. Now then, the reason that I have come by way of this town, is to tell you what happened after you left Kagara. This boy, nine days after your departure, was stolen by some kidnapper. A very thorough search was made, but nothing more was heard of him. At this time I was not at home. I had gone to a village to see a friend of mine who was unwell. When I returned I met with this news. But we have heard from one of the Chief's servants, called Ahmadu, that he is certain that he saw Umar in Kano City, in the compound of a certain head slave of the Chief of Kano, who is called Gumuzu. Moreover, he said that he had heard this Gumuzu and an Arab by the name of Abdulkarim talking, saying something about him wanting to redeem the boy and take him off to Egypt, to give him to his wife, that is to say, he was to become like their son. This is the news that I can give you concerning Umar, and this is the reason that made me come by way of this town. So now you must bear patiently what God has willed, and remember that patience is best of all.'

My mother just kept silent. After a long time she said, 'You are right, anyone in this world, if he does not exercise patience, surely he will know a thousand sorrows. God will lighten all our troubles.'

When Buhari had finished giving her this news, he went out and left her talking with Amina. They talked until midnight, and then mother got up and went home. On arriving she told her mother and father what had happened, and they both exclaimed, 'God is mighty!'

When dawn broke mother returned to Amina and the rest to spend the day with them. While she was there, a younger brother of hers came running, saying that he had been sent from the compound to call her: she had a guest from Zazzau way. She got up at once, went back to the compound, and found that it was Isa, the man whom Makau had sent to bring his family to Makarfi. She made him welcome, and brought him water to drink. Then she went and informed her father that it was her husband's servant. At once a hut was swept out for him, and she took him to it. After he had sat down and rested a while, he said to her, 'Do you recognise me?'

She replied, 'Why, until my dying day I shall never forget you.'

He said to her, 'The fact is, Makau is insisting, he wants you to make haste and go back and join him together with the boy. He says that we should start off at once, you following hard in my footsteps.'

Mother said, 'Very well.' Then she told him all that had happened since they had last seen each other. Isa marvelled greatly at what God had decreed.

When they had finished this conversation, she took him to her parents, so that he might tell them Makau's message with his own mouth. Isa told them everything, and then went back to his hut and lay down because of the heat of the sun which he had endured on his journey to Fatika. As for her, after she had parted from Isa, she returned joyfully to Amina and the rest. She told them of the good fortune which had befallen her. They all became so happy that they almost forgot about my being lost. When mother was about to return home, she said a final farewell to Amina and her companions, because they were to depart early in the morning. When they had said goodbye she returned to her compound. At first light Amina and the rest of her party rose and set out for Hausa country.

As for my mother, as soon as she returned to the compound, she began to make ready to join her husband. Five days after Amina and the rest had left, mother and Isa also set out. They made the journey uneventfully, and after four days, that is on the fifth day, they were at Makarfi.

When they arrived they found that Makau was not in the compound. He had gone to inspect a new farm in the open country beyond the town. Isa took mother into the compound to the other women, went himself to his compound and washed, and changed his clothes. Then he came out and went off to Makau in the country, and let him know that he had returned safely. Makau wasted no time, but there and then got up and hastened home. He arrived and entered his compound, laughing happily to himself and full of joy at the arrival of his wife. He showed her to her hut and she went in.

After she had rested and recovered herself fully, the first thing he asked her was for news of me. She told him that I had disappeared. After this he asked her more questions, and she told him everything that she knew. Then dismay seized him, and he became entirely distraught.

These then are the things which happened to my mother. But at the end of them all, she kept a stout heart, for she knew that God is One. If God willed, somehow or other she would get to where I was, if she did not die in the attempt.

I AM SOLD TO AN ARAB

At the time when Gumuzu captured us, there was a caravan of Arabs in Kano, who had come to buy slaves and take them back to their country. Most of them used to be on friendly terms with the head slaves of the Chief, because whenever they came it was they who enabled them to obtain slaves. They did not arrive in all seasons; there were specially appointed times for their coming. And each time that they came and bought slaves, when they were about to return to their own country, they would make an arrangement with these friends of theirs, that they should collect a certain number of slaves for them before they returned again. Among these Arabs Gumuzu had a friend called Abdulkarim, from a certain city in Egypt.

One day we were sitting there, after we had been with Gumuzu for exactly two years, when I saw a certain tall light-skinned man with a long beard and a moustache, coming towards him. On his approach I saw that Gumuzu got up from his carpet and invited him to sit on it, saying to him, 'Welcome, welcome!' After they had finished greeting each other he called me and told me to go into the compound and fetch some water for this guest. I went and brought him some *fura*[1] water with honey. I came back and knelt before the guest, and offered it to him, and he accepted it and drank. After he had drunk the water he said, 'Praise be to God', then he turned to Gumuzu and asked him, 'How is this, I don't know this boy, is it your son?'

Gumuzu said 'No, no, I'll tell you how I came by him, together with his father and mother at one and the same time.'

They went on talking for a long time, while I remained with them, and then each one returned to his compound. The guest's compound was near to Gumuzu's. The Chief had given him a place to live on his first arrival, so that he could lodge there whenever he came. Whenever food was prepared, I had to put it on my head and take it to his lodging. Eventually we got to know each other well, on account of the food which I always took him. Sometimes, when I brought it to him, he would ask me whether I liked him. When I went away he would take hold of me and stroke my head, blessing me. Sometimes, when I was about to return home, he would fetch some dates, and some other kind of food, and give them to me.

He treated me like this for about sixteen days. On the seventeenth day I saw Gumuzu meet him, and they set out for the palace. When they were about to leave Abdulkarim asked Gumuzu whether he would agree that I should go and sit in his house and look after his property, pending their return. Gumuzu called me, and told me. I went to Abdulkarim's compound and sat in his house, while they went off. From the time that they left in the morning, they did not return again until after midday prayer. I was sitting there in his hut, when I began to hear the hubbub of men shouting, and the voice of Gumuzu. Before long, I saw Abdulkarim come into the hut. I greeted him, and he said to me, 'All right, go home now.'

1 A thin gruel made of flour mixed with water or milk.

On leaving his hut, I looked about me, and then I saw slaves bound together by a leather thong round the neck, exposed in the open sun. When I took a closer look among these slaves, I saw this mother and father of mine, with whom I had been captured and brought here from the farm. At that moment my heart failed me, and I became much afraid. When I saw this, I bent my head and passed by, tears running down from my eyes. I went home and was given food, but although I was feeling hungry I had to leave it. I could think of nothing except those slaves. Whenever I lowered my head I could see them. Oh dear, I was like someone who has just heard the news that his father and mother had died. I became confused, and I felt that there was no comfort for me in the whole world. I just felt I had to go to my foster-mother's hut, and I lay down there, like someone suffering from a fatal illness. I sat silently, with my head raised, gazing at the roof of the hut, just thinking.

While I was deep in thought I heard my master Gumuzu enter the compound. When he came in, I heard him call my name, saying, 'Where's so-and-so?' When I heard that, I jumped with fright and said, 'Here I am.' I went to him and he took my hand and led me to the compound where Abdulkarim was staying. We arrived there, went into the compound and found him reading the Koran, from *Surat al-baqara*.[1] As we entered he shut the book and said to Gumuzu, 'So you've found him at last?'

He answered, 'Yes, though he never has been one to wander off, like the rest of the boys.'

Then they began to talk in a language that I was unable to understand properly. Some words I could understand; others were as if in an unknown tongue.[2] When they had finished talking I heard Gumuzu say, 'Abdulkarim, you do me an injury when you part me from this boy, for all the time that I have been concerned with boys, I have never seen one as sensible and as given to minding

1 'The Chapter of the Cow', the second chapter of the Koran.
2 The language in which they were speaking was Arabic. Umar was able to understand certain words because there is a very large number of Arabic loan words in Hausa.

his own business as this one. For you know, ever since the day that I was fortunate enough to bring him to this compound, I have never heard any one of my wives, or any kinsman of mine say a cross word to the boy.'

Abdulkarim replied, 'This is the kind of character which the Arabs like; any man anywhere in the world, if he has not got character, even if he is a somebody, whether he be white, yellow, or black, is no better than an animal. For good sense, insight, and wisdom certainly never came from anything other than an excellent character.'

On hearing these words, I began to think to myself, 'Abdulkarim must surely be going to take me to the country of the Arabs.'

As I was turning this over in my mind Gumuzu turned to me and said, 'Umar, here is Abdulkarim asking a favour of me: he's wanting you. Now of course this does not mean that he wants you to become his slave. What he wants is, if you are agreeable and you think you will be able to live with him, that you should become his son, for he has no son, not even a kinsman's son living with him. I for my part have agreed that you should go with him, and now it's just your consent that we are waiting for.'

After he had finished, I just raised my head, imagining how far it must be to Abdulkarim's country and thinking of my natural mother living without knowing where God had led me. At this moment the world about me became black with sorrow, and without my realising it my tears began to flow. On seeing this, Abdulkarim asked me whether this meant I did not like him? I replied that it was not this at all, but that I did not want to leave my own country. If I went with him, when should I return home? He told me that every year that he came, he would certainly bring me with him, for me to see my own countrymen.

I said, 'Very well, I agree', lest they should think that I was lacking in modesty after they had praised me. After this conversation was quite concluded, and I had agreed, Gumuzu told me to go home. When I got up to go, Abdulkarim brought a big block of sugar and gave me, together with some unusually sweet dried dates.

I knelt and accepted them. Then I got up again and wrapped them in a large loin cloth of *saki* cloth, which Gumuzu had brought for me. I went out and made for home. I reached the compound with my heart breaking, and I went to my foster-mother's hut and collapsed upon her bed. Then I leaned against the partition wall of the hut, and crouched with my head on my knees. I really was a pitiful sight. When she saw this she burst into tears and asked me what had happened to me. I told her the whole story from beginning to end. She began to weep, saying, 'Never mind Umar, just keep on remembering in your heart God is King.'

We talked on until God brought Gumuzu to tell her himself that I was to go to Egypt with a certain Arab friend of his.

She said, 'Well, may God spare our lives.'

He said, 'Amen.'

And so it went on until the day, about seventeen days after this conversation, that Abdulkarim decided to set out, for he had already completed his preparations, his needs were supplied, and he had bought as many slaves as he could buy. In addition to these slaves, he had bought some lengths of black turban, black cloths, and similar goods to use to buy provisions for the road. After he had finished his preparations on the day before he was due to set out, he sent someone to call me, and I went to him. He told me that he had completed his preparations, that he was going to set out tomorrow early in the morning, and that I should go and bid farewell to my friends, and also to the women of the compound who had looked after me—that is to say, Gumuzu's family.

I said, 'Very well.' I got up, returned to the compound and said goodbye to the whole company. Then I folded up my little sleeping mat and carrying it under my arm I made for his compound, to sleep there so that I should not be late. I found him sitting there, around about the time for evening prayer, after he had counted his slaves. And moreover, there were ten others bound together on one side, which the Chief had sent him as a parting gift. That night he made me go into the hut with him, and we slept together on one rug until first light.

WE LEAVE KANO CITY

As dawn broke I heard them blowing something like a horn, and beating a gong. On hearing this I became flustered and jumped up in a fright. I roused Abdulkarim and told him. He told me that these were indications to the travellers, to let them know that the rest of their companions were ready, and were about to start. At once he opened the door and went out. He went and fetched his white Bactrian camel. Then he went to the pound where the slaves were exposed in the open air, like sheep, and roused them, and we set out.

We left Kano City at dawn on Saturday, the third of the month of Ramadan,[1] in the year thirteen hundred of the Hijra[2] of our Prophet Muhammad—may God bless him and give him peace. Those travelling to Egypt used to assemble at the gate of the town first. I have forgotten the name of the gate now. When the assembly was complete, the signal to depart was given. Before we left the gate the Chief of Kano sent us about fifty horsemen to escort us.

When we were about to start my master called me, and lifted me up and put me in front of him upon his camel. We travelled on and I did not know the direction in which we were heading, and until the sun had risen and set again we did not halt. To cut a long story short, from the time that we left Kano I do not think that we stayed at any town, except Kuka.[3] After leaving Kuka we stopped only on an open plain, thick with coarse sand. There was not a

---

1 The ninth month of the Mohammedan year, during all the daylight hours of which strict fasting is observed.
2 The Arabic word *hijra* means 'Flight' or 'Emigration'. The Mohammedan era commenced on 16 July, A.D. 622, the day on which Mohammed left Mecca, to make his home in Medina.
3 A city in Bornu to the west of Lake Chad. See Boahen, op. cit., map facing page 102. It was a main staging point for the caravans taking the eastern route.

58

single compound in the place, only some traces of grass huts; here it was that the caravans used to halt to make final preparations and take on water before entering the great Sahara. We spent two days here, and the Arabs spent all their time overhauling their weapons, and the water skins were filled and loaded onto camels. Before we set out a certain elderly Arab came to Abdulkarim, advising him that he should tell his people to be prepared, because the place that we were about to enter was a dangerous one. Then I began to be afraid, thinking that perhaps they might be going to fight, and that this was why they had got ready their guns and swords.

After a short while the gong was sounded, and we all set out together at sunset, and entered the Sahara. Gracious me! Here in this desert I saw some amazing things, and what is more, I felt the fear of God, and I certainly learned the truth of what the lion said to the hyena—'Man is a thing to be feared!'

From the time that we began to enter the desert, I saw no large tree. Wherever you looked, as far as the eye could reach, you could see nothing but sand. There was no rain, let alone any fertility to be found in this place. There was wind, but not like the wind in this country. The wind there brought with it nothing but sand.

Any man who knows what the wind of the Sahara is like will have no wish to be caught in it. For if the wind rises out there, when you look you would think it was a storm. A certain Arab, a friend of mine, told me that sometimes when this wind catches a caravan of people, it makes them panic and lose their way, and they all scatter in the sand. And however wide the road in the Sahara, when this wind blows over the place, the road is lost. Yes, and when we entered this place I was overcome with pity for the slaves. Whenever I looked at them, I would see them toiling along through the sand, bent double, their buttocks swaying from side to side. O dear me, you know, it is a hard thing for a man who is used to the solid earth to have to walk through sand.

So we made our way on through the sand, day after day. But not

59

to make a long story of it, from the time that we set out from the place where we stopped and drew water, we did not find water again until after we had been travelling for three days. Then we came to a little town inhabited by some Buzu[1] by the side of some small wells in the sand. Now at this town I saw an amazing thing. All the men of the town, young and old, were each wearing a black turban of about three cubits in length. And of each of those who was wearing a turban, not one had a cap.[2] And most of them, when they wore the turban, pulled it down over their faces so as to veil themselves with it.[3] And the women of the town too, each of them had a little piece of cloth with which she veiled her face. I had heard tell that these people were very cantankerous. I myself saw evidence of this when I heard them talking, for whatever they had to say, it always sounded as if they were quarrelling.

WE DO SOME TRADING

When we reached this town of which I have told you, we halted beside some wells, drew water, drank, and each one of us washed. Shortly afterwards I saw the townspeople, women and men, streaming out towards us. And no sooner had I seen this than I saw every single one of our merchants undo his loads and take out black turbans and cloths of the kind made in Kano. Then I saw pandemonium let loose, nothing but people everywhere, haggling with each other. These merchants went on trading until sundown, and then about the time of evening prayer, I saw each one take his loads and tie them up. Then, as dusk approached, they beat the gong and we set off.

We carried on through this desert, and did not come out of it until after two months and eight days. Then one day, after we had

1 Serfs of the Tuareg who wear the *litham*, or Tuareg face veil.
2 In contrast, it is customary among the Hausa to wear the turban wound round a fez cap.
3 The bottom fold of the turban is drawn down across the bridge of the nose, thus veiling the lower half of the face.

covered a long hard journey, we arrived at a certain town in the country of Egypt, to the west of the Nile, called Ber Kufa. This town was Abdulkarim's home, where I was to remain for many a long year. When we were nearly there Abdulkarim told me that this was their town, and that his own house was near to the place I could see in the distance. We moved on a little way and found ourselves in a town the like of which I had never seen since the day my mother bore me. On entering the town, after we had passed three houses, we arrived at Abdulkarim's house. We stopped there, together with his slaves, and the rest of the people continued on towards their own houses.

By now the slaves had become utterly exhausted. They were brought water and food, but they were not able to touch either, because of fatigue. As for me, when we arrived Abdulkarim took me to his wife and left me with her, and went out. After the slaves were fully rested and had recovered, they fell upon the food, as though they were locusts who had come upon a farm where the guinea corn had begun to sprout, and fell upon it, stripping it bare. Abdulkarim sat by the slaves until they had quite finished eating, then he entered the house and found me sitting with his wife, talking to her in Hausa, for she knew this language. The reason was that since he had begun to trade in Hausaland he had taken her with him at least once, and they had spent about three years in Kano. He came in and told her all about me, and what he intended to do with me. She was delighted.

After seven days I had become quite used to Abdulkarim's wife, and then one day he said he wished to go down to the sea[1] to sell his slaves. Originally he had set out with eighty slaves, but twenty-five had died on the road. Before he set out, he told his wife that after he had left, she should take me to a certain teacher, a neighbour of his, so that I could take up the study of the Koran, and he called me and told me this, and then he left. He set out in the morning and on the evening of the same day his wife Zainab took me to

1 Probably the Red Sea, from where the slaves would then be shipped to Arabia.

Shaikh Mas'ud, under whom I was to study the Koran. She told him everything that her husband had said. When she had told him, we returned home together, and she said that I should not start my studies until the following day, if God spared us.

Early the next morning she gave me a new gown, a cap and trousers, and also some breakfast. After I had finished breakfast, she said that I should set out for the school. I set out and went to Shaikh Mas'ud's house, and began my studies. Gracious me, it soon reached the point that, once I had begun to study, I did not want to go home at all, except for my food. Before long I was reciting passages aloud, and the whole thing became for me like a game of draughts,[1] for wherever I was, you would hear me reciting. Before a month was out I was able to read from a reading board. Before Abdulkarim returned from the sea I was able to recite by heart from *Surat al-fatihah*[2] to *Surat al-a'la*.[3]

On this day, the seventh of the month, three days before the tenth of Muharram,[4] Abdulkarim returned. On his arrival Zainab told him all about me, and he was delighted indeed. He had a ram caught and slaughtered and gave alms on my behalf.[5] From that day on, whatever I said I needed, there and then it would be given me. There was no sort of clothes that I didn't wear.

When the year came round, Abdulkarim made up his mind to return to Kano. He said that we should go together because of the promise which he had made me. When I heard this I longed for the time to come for me to go and visit my country. After we had quite made ready, someone brought him news of what had hap-

1 The Hausa game of *dara* resembles draughts or backgammon. It is played with beans or cowrie shells, sometimes on a board containing a number of holes, sometimes with holes in the sand. Denham witnessed the game in Bornu. 'Here they talk, and sometimes play a game resembling chess, with beans, and twelve holes made in the sand. The Arabs have a game similar to this, which they play with camel's dung in the desert, but the Bornouese are more skilful.' *Travels*, iii, 183.
2 'The Opening Chapter'—the first chapter of the Koran.
3 'The Chapter of the Most High'—the eighty-seventh chapter.
4 The first month of the Mohammedan year. The tenth of Muharram is a festival in commemoration of the death of al-Husayn at the Battle of Karbala, A.D. 680.
5 It is an occasion for thanksgiving when a Muslim boy has successfully memorised part of the Koran.

pened in the Sudan. This was that Muhammad Ahmad[1] had risen against Egypt, and had claimed to be the Mahdi.[2] The people of the Sudan had all followed him. An expeditionary force had been sent against him from Egypt.

When Abdulkarim heard this he said that it would be better for us to wait and see what was going to happen, because this was the way we were going to go. Now at this time everybody thought that the affair would not last long, and that it would be concluded there and then, and we could start. We were thinking thus, and then news came that the war had worsened. The Mahdi's people had been victorious, and the whole country was in disorder. Another expeditionary force was sent from Egypt, but the affair had already worsened. When we heard this news, there was no chance of making the journey, and we had perforce to stay where we were.

Now you know what a boy is like, as the days went by I began to forget our country and my kinsfolk, and even my mother. I continued to study until, after about two years, I had completed the reading of the Koran. I completed it on Wednesday, the nineteenth of the month of Muharram. On this day a feast took place, the like of which I shall probably never see again. Early in the morning three cows were caught and slaughtered, two camels were stuck, and about nine sheep and turkeys slaughtered. The food which was prepared in our house, and that which was contributed from other households was unlimited. Abdulkarim went into his room and brought out a gown of the type worn by the Arabs, excellently worked, gleaming like silver, and trousers from Tunis embroidered as far as the waist band, and a kind of shirt made of silk, and a fez cap with a tassel of white silk, and a yellow turban. All these things

1 Muhammad Ahmad b. ‘Abdullāh was the famous Mahdi of the Sudan. He was born in A.D. 1843, and claimed to be related to the Prophet Mohammed. He initiated a movement of religious reform, and in A.D. 1881 he rose in revolt against the government of Egypt. He was at the height of his power in 1884, and dominated the whole of Kordufan and the Bahr al-Ghazal area. In 1885 he took Khartoum, and his followers killed General Gordon, who was defending the city. Muhammad Ahmad died in 1885, and was succeeded by the Khalifa ‘Abdullāh. The Mahdiya, as his movement was called, was finally defeated by Kitchener, in 1898.
2 The Arabic word *mahdi* means ‘Messiah’.

he gave me to put on. When I had put them on, he said that I should proceed in front of him to the school, where the important malams were gathered, in order that I might give a brief reading from the Koran for them to hear, and that they might then pray for me. I went in front until we reached the school. We sat down, and everybody just gazed at me in wonderment. Shaihu Mas'ud brought some papers, two sheets of the Koran, and gave them to me to read, as a test. Everyone then sat back and fell silent. They listened attentively, and I began to read. I read those sheets perfectly, without even the smallest error. When I had finished, throughout the whole assembly people exclaimed, 'Praise be to God!' Prayers were said for me, and then they began to share out the food.

A few days after I had completed the reading of the Koran, my master Abdulkarim brought some books on the religious sciences and gave them to me, together with some others containing prayers, and yet others containing remedies.[1] I accepted them, and took them to Shaihu Mas'ud.

When I gave them to him, he accepted them, and spread them out on his carpet. He picked up one of them, *al-Ashmawiya*,[2] and gave it to me, and said that this was the one I should start with, for this was the first book which teaches a man thoroughly concerning religion. I started the book, and before you could say, 'What!' I had read it completely. Within a few years I had come near to being the next in rank after Shaihu Mas'ud himself in the city of Ber Kufa. From that time people began to call me Shaihu Umar, and many people from the towns of Egypt kept coming to visit me. When they came they would express astonishment, saying that here I was, a black man, and yet God had given me abundant insight and understanding. Thus I continued, and then, when Shaihu Mas'ud died, there was no doubt about it, it was I who was chosen in his place as Imam, and it was I who instructed all his students.

1 Traditional Muslim medicine was based largely on the practice of the Prophet Mohammed, and was regarded as part of religious science.
2 A work on Islamic law by al-Ashmāwī, a Muslim jurist of the fifteenth century A.D.

But away in my own country my mother, ever since she had learned that I had been kidnapped, had not had a moment's peace of mind. Whenever she was alone she kept saying in her heart that if God willed, in whatever town I might be, there she would go. From the time that we had been separated, the food which she ate did her no good. She wasted away and became as thin as a skeleton, and as pale as a ghost, and quite lost her good looks. Makau did much for her, so that she should stop thinking about me, but all to no avail, and in the end he became tired and gave up.

Then one day, after I had been separated from her for about a year, she went and asked Makau to give her leave to go to wherever I might be in the whole world, so that she could see me and then return. At first Makau would not consent, but when she insisted, he agreed. He brought cowries and clothes in large quantities, and gave them to her, and she set out and journeyed to Kano. On her arrival in the city, she asked after the compound of Gumuzu, and she was taken there, and there she lodged. She asked him for news of where I was, and he told her. He did not hide anything from her. He told her the name of the country in which I was, and of the town, and the name of my master. When she heard this news she sighed, and said, 'Praise be to God.' Then she asked how she could get to where I was.

Gumuzu answered her, 'You have certainly come at a good moment, for there are some caravans which are about to leave for there within three days. But these caravans are in two sections. One section is going to Murzuk; the other to where your son is.'

Two days after this conversation she set out for the market, enquiring where the caravans leaving on the morrow were. She was directed to the caravans going to Murzuk.[1] Now in these caravans was a certain merchant of Kano who was going there, called Ado. On her arrival at the place where the caravans were assembled, she

---

[1] A Saharan city situated in the Fezzan (Boahen, op. cit., map facing page 102).

went up to him and knelt down, asking him about the departure. He told her, 'tomorrow', and then he asked her, 'Are you going to join this party?'

She replied, 'Yes, I want to go and find my son, who is in a certain town called Ber Kufa, in Egypt.'

When Ado heard this, he plotted in his heart to cheat my mother into travelling with him, so that he could pass her off as his wife, and among his wives, as his slave girl. He said to her, 'So, that's splendid, go to your compound and fetch your loads. Oh, but God has certainly granted you good fortune to have found me travelling in this party. Come, stay with me until God brings us safely there, for our route takes us past the very town which you mentioned.'

When my mother heard these words, she returned to her lodging, collected her loads, and handed them over to him, saying that she entrusted herself to his care, since God had brought them together in this way. After she had brought her loads to him that evening, early next morning they set out. They journeyed on. One day they would spend in this town; on the morrow they would set out again, and so they continued until they reached Ghat.[1] Here they decided to spend several days so as to trade. So far, my mother did not know what Ado was intending to do with her. The rest of the people in the caravan, when they saw her with him, thought that she was a wife of his, for they noticed that on the road he was showing signs of being jealous of her.

On the day before they were to set out, Ado went to market to buy some provisions, and then my mother came upon a Kano woman, a slave of a certain Arab. They sat and talked, and the woman asked my mother why she had left home. She told her, and the woman beat her breast and said, 'Dear God, this man has deceived you. You left the road to Egypt way back at Kano!'

My mother simply sat silent, not knowing what to say. After a while she said, 'Alas! What am I to do! We have already come a

1 A Saharan city north-west of Murzuk (Boahen, op. cit., map facing page 102).

long way, and it is not possible to turn back. What is more, the cowries which I brought from home are now finished.'

The other woman said, 'If you take my advice, don't show him that you have realised what he is up to, and then, on the day that God brings you to Murzuk, lodge a complaint against him.'

THEY ARRIVE AT MURZUK

Ado returned from the market about the time of evening prayer, and when dusk fell they set out. They journeyed on, day after day, until one day God brought them to Murzuk. The Arabs and the others who were in the caravan each went to his own house, and Ado too had a house in the town, and he took my mother and her loads and they went there and lodged. After two days Ado said to my mother, 'Don't think that I am not going to take you to Ber Kufa. The fact is, when I've finished buying up what I need, I want to pass that way, and then we can go back together.'

He went on talking, and as for her, she did not say a word to him until he had finished and was silent. She simply ignored him until she saw that he had fully made ready to return home, and then she spoke up, 'I am going to lodge a complaint about you with the cadi.'

Ado replied, 'All right, go to the cadi by all means, and let us see whether he can take you away from me!'

Then Ado went off out and did not stop until he arrived at the cadi's court. He said to him, 'It's about a certain female slave whom I brought from Hausaland, but I find she has taken leave of her senses, she has no intention of accompanying me when I return, for she says she means to lodge a complaint against me with you.'

The cadi said, 'I see; we'll see about that when she comes.'

While Ado was on his way home, she set out to make her complaint against him at the cadi's court. The cadi asked her what had brought her. She replied, 'I am complaining about a man called Ado. Away back in Kano he said that I should follow him, and that he would take me to my son, and now we have been on the road for a long time, and I see no sign that he intends to take me there. And I know no-one who can show me the road.'

The cadi asked her, 'In what town is your son?'

She said, 'In Ber Kufa, in Egypt.'

When the cadi heard that, he thought that she must surely be out of her senses, and he said, 'If that is what it is all about, then it is a simple matter! Just you stay here in my house until I find someone who is going there.'

When it was evening the cadi sent someone to summon Ado, fetched a small sum of money which he gave him, and said, 'That is all, the case is closed. I wish you a safe journey.'

There my mother was in the cadi's house, when a man from Tripoli whose name was Ahmad, saw her and said to the cadi that he wanted to redeem her and take her away. They did a bit of bargaining and he paid the cadi.

The cadi called her and said to her, 'Here we are, I have found a man who will take you to Ber Kufa. I am going to put you in his company for him to take you to where your son is.' She was overjoyed at this, and thanked him.

The next day they set out and travelled until one day God brought them safely to Tripoli, in the evening. This man went straight to his own house. When dawn broke he called his head slave woman and said to her, 'Here is a companion whom I have obtained for you, whatever work there is to do, she is to take her share with you.'

When my mother heard this, she said, 'A'a, master, the cadi at Murzuk put me in your company for you to take me to my son, and now are you saying that I am your slave?'

Ahmad answered, 'Never, that is not so at all, what I did was to redeem you from the cadi at Murzuk.'

She replied, 'Very well.' She went away saying, 'Ah me! All the trouble in the world has come upon me; as for the future, may God be kind to me.'

She continued as usual, and did not show any sign that she was upset, until she saw that they had got used to her. One day she was sent to market, whereupon she went directly to the cadi's court, and made her complaint. The cadi had Ahmad summoned. When he came she told him her story. He replied, 'She is lying. The fact is that I redeemed her from the cadi at Murzuk.'

The cadi said, 'Very well, you, woman, go back to his household and stay there. I will write a letter to the cadi at Murzuk, whatever he says, when the answer comes back, I will send for you both.'

When they had left the cadi wrote a letter and sent it to the cadi at Murzuk. In due course the answer came back, the cadi had them summoned, and he said to her, 'I have got an answer from the cadi at Murzuk; he says you are lying, the fact of the matter is that he sold you to him. Now go away and stay where you are and serve your master.'

She said to the cadi, 'I understand. As for the future, I leave it to God to judge between us.' Ahmad paid his respects and departed with his slave.

When they had returned to the house he said to her, 'Since you have behaved to me in this way, I shall not leave you at liberty. I will tie you up until such time as you come to your senses.' Then he had her put in chains. All the hardest housework, she had to do it, and she was only given food at irregular intervals. For her part, because of her unhappiness and brooding on her misfortunes she became completely worn out, and she lost her good looks. When she finished work she would just sit down and weep.

When he saw this he said to himself, 'This slave is thoroughly disobedient, and beating is the only cure for it.' Time and again he beat her, but despite this she did not change her attitude. He went on punishing her in this way for about a year. But for her part, all this hardship that she suffered did not trouble her, for what always lay heavy on her mind was her failure to find her son, until finally she became worn out and could no longer work, but could only weep.

When her master saw that there was nothing more that he could do with her, he said, 'Surely if I go on like this with this useless slave woman, I shall kill her and lose all my money.' He released her from the chains, but despite this her heart would not mend, and she declined even further.

I HAVE A BAD DREAM

While I was enjoying myself at Ber Kufa nothing was too much for me, and I forgot everything about Hausaland. And then one day after evening prayer, I got up and performed my ablutions. I took up the Koran, looking at it as was always my custom, when sleep came over me. I had not been asleep long before I had a dream. There I was upon a high rock at the mouth of a large cave. In the cave were a lioness and her cub. Now originally I had been with some hunters who were hunting lion. After a little while, when I turned my head, I saw there was no-one upon the rock except I, the lioness, and her cub. Then suddenly she came out of the cave and made for the thick bush to hunt for food. Then, after she had been gone a little while, I saw her come back and go into the cave. As soon as she had gone in, she turned and came running out again, roaring and growling, for she couldn't see her cub. She began to pace round the rock crying out, but she could not find it. Then, my goodness, I began to see a confused jumble of all sorts of things. Just before I woke up, I saw my mother at the mouth of the lion's cave, calling my name.

When I saw this I was frightened, and I got up, bewildered and confused in my thoughts. I began to ponder on this dream, and for a long time I did not disclose it to anyone. Then I could not bear it any longer, and I went and told it to my master, Abdulkarim. I said to him, 'Today I am unhappy. The thought that keeps coming to my mind is that my mother is seeking me. Moreover, I realise that my thoughts are back in my own country, but I do not know how I can manage to see her once again.'

Then Abdulkarim said, 'I myself have been wondering how I can manage to return to Hausaland, because this thing that we thought little of has become serious. The whole country of the Sudan has become unsettled. The Mahdi's party have conquered the country, and I see no sign that Egypt will be able to regain control. What is more, all the goods which I got ready to sell over there, are here, lying uselessly in store. But yesterday I heard from one of my kinsmen who had been to trade in Tripoli, that caravans are going to Hausaland by that route.[1] Moreover, it is a main route and is better than the one which we followed. So what I have decided is that I will go down to the sea[2] and take a boat for Tripoli, from there I will find a caravan going to Hausaland. Now then, God willing, I will take you with me, and I will take you to the town where your mother is. But I have one condition which I want to make. I want you to promise me that if we go, we will return together. If you think that when we arrive in your country, you will treat me as ungrateful people do, then tell me in good time, so that I may know. I also want you to be sure in your mind, supposing you decide that if you go, you will not come back, that this is all right. I shall not press you. For you know that I have taken you as my son, and you are the joy of my life.'

I listened attentively until Abdulkarim had finished what he had to say, then I said to him, 'Today, in this whole world I know that I have no other father than you, you brought me up, and you established me among men, how then do you suppose that I should run away from you? You know well that even though there are some to whom you do good, and they return evil, yet I am not that sort. Were I to do that to you, God would surely call me to account.'

I sat and talked with Abdulkarim until nearly midday. Then he told me to go back to my house because my students had begun to assemble. When I went I found that many of my students had gathered beneath the tree at the gate of my compound, and each

1 That is, the Tripoli–Fezzan–Bornu route.
2 The Mediterranean. As we shall see, they boarded a ship at Alexandria.

one had opened his book and was going over the lesson. I went into the house and washed, and then I came out and began to teach. After I had finished teaching we got up, and each one performed his ablutions,[1] and I went out in front, and we said our prayers.[2] When we had finished prayer, I told them that in that present month Abdulkarim said that we were to set out and I was to visit my home, God willing. When I had said this I saw that they were not happy, and I asked them the reason. They said that what they were afraid of was that maybe, when I went home, I should not come back again. I assured them that this was not so at all.

On the ninth day of the month in which the old people keep the fast,[3] we finished our preparations and set out. We embarked on a boat, and followed the course of the Nile until we arrived at Cairo. From there we went straight to Alexandria, where we found a big ship. A few days later we arrived in Tripoli.

When we disembarked from the ship Abdulkarim enquired from somebody, saying that he wanted him to tell him whether there was anyone in the town who was in the habit of trading with Hausaland.[4]

The man said to him, 'In this town the best-known person is Ahmad.' He took us to Ahmad's house. Ahmad made us welcome, lodged us, and showed us great hospitality.

After we had rested that day, Abdulkarim arrived in conversation with Ahmad, enquiring from him about the route. Ahmad told him all he knew. Abdulkarim said, 'If God spares us, tomorrow I will set out.'

Then Ahmad said to him, 'I have a certain female slave, a native of Hausaland, whom I purchased and brought here from Murzuk

1 Before each of the prescribed prayers the Muslim must carry out ceremonial ablution.
2 When a number of persons are gathered together, prayer is said communally. The *imam*, or prayer-leader, stands in front of the congregation with his back towards them, facing the east, and leads prayer. The congregation arrange themselves in ranks, also facing east, and follow the *imam*.
3 The month of Muharram, in which old people observe a voluntary fast.
4 Monteil mentioned the Arabs of Tripoli as among those having established a monopoly of the trans-Saharan trade. See Introduction, page 15, note 2.

last year, but she has a thoroughly bad character, and since I bought her she has not been of the least use to me, but has simply gone from bad to worse for thinking about her own country. If I do not get rid of her now, I shall surely lose my money. Now since it is your trade, and what's more you speak their language, perhaps you will know how to cure her, for all I want is to be rid of her.'

Abdulkarim said, 'Where is she?'

Ahmad went into the house and called her and she came out. When she came out Abdulkarim said, '*Sannunki!*'[1]

When she heard him speak to her in her own language she threw herself down before him, weeping. He asked her, 'What is the matter with you? And from what town do you come?'

She said, 'I am a Fatika woman, my husband is there in a town called Makarfi, it's there that I left him.'

He said, 'What happened that you came here?'

She began to tell him how she had left the town, looking for her son, and how she had been tricked and sold into slavery, until eventually she had arrived in this household. When she had finished he said to her, 'What do you want now?'

She said, 'There is nothing I want so much as to fulfil the purpose which brought me away from my home, to succeed in seeing my son, and then, if so be it, let me die.'

When he heard this he wondered at the strength of her character, and he said, 'Do you know the name of the town in which your son is?'

She said, 'Yes, for I was told there was some man who took him to his own town in Egypt, and the name of the town was Ber Kufa.'

He said, 'Ber Kufa! What was the name of his master?'

She said, 'They said his name was Abdulkarim.'

He said, 'Abdulkarim! What was the name of the boy?'

She said, 'Umar.'

When he heard this he said, 'God is great. God is the One who

1 See page 40 note 1. *ki* is the Hausa third person singular feminine pronoun.

disposes according to His will! You are fortunate, God has looked upon you, today your troubles are over.'

Then he turned to Ahmad and said to him, 'How much shall I give you to redeem her?'

Ahmad replied, 'Give me what you like.'

Abdulkarim went and fetched money[1] and gave it to him. Then he called me and said to her. 'Here is the one whom you are seeking. What is more, I am Abdulkarim.'

MY MOTHER SEES ME

She looked at me and said, 'Umar! Is it you?' Then she burst into tears.

As for me, I was standing there in amazement, when I felt my body go cold. I asked Abdulkarim, 'Who is this? Why is she crying?'

Then my mother answered and said, 'I am the mother who bore you. For many years now I have been seeking you, and at last God has brought us together.' Then she fell upon me and embraced me, and I was lost for words.

Then Abdulkarim said we should go to our lodging place. When we had gone there, she recovered herself and began to tell me the story of all that had happened to her. And I for my part told her what had happened to me.

Then I said, 'Now, God willing, I shall take you home.'

She replied, 'Alas! I am worn out. I know that I shall never return home, but now that I have seen you, this is enough for me. As for you, may God bring you home, so that you may see the rest of your kinsfolk.'

I said, 'Do not talk like that, God will make it all easy for us.'

But alas, her strength was already exhausted because of what she

---

1 In this case not cowries, since these were not currency in North Africa. According to Barth, Timbuctu appears to have been the most northerly point of the cowrie exchange area. In North Africa both silver dollars and the gold *mithkal* were current.

had suffered, and then on top of that the joy of seeing me had been too much for her. From that time she did not leave her bed again. Indeed it was God who had allowed us to see each other once again. After a few days, she died. We buried her. Seven days after she was buried, we set out. For my part, I simply travelled on, but my heart was full of thoughts about what had happened to me. The days went by, and nothing untoward happened to us on the way until we reached Murzuk.

When we halted at Murzuk we did not find any caravans going on any further, and so we remained there for some months; then we found some caravans and continued on our way.

WE PROCEED WITH OUR JOURNEY

When we left Murzuk we travelled on for about three months, until God brought us safely to a small village called Muhtad. On arrival we split up, asking for news of the route which we were to follow. Whoever we asked, we heard only that the road was unsafe, there was nothing but highway robbery and inter-tribal wars. When we heard this, the leaders of our caravan assembled to take council as to what was to be done. At this meeting their opinions differed. Some said we should go back; others that we should go on. Dear me, in these discussions I realised how fond people are of wealth. Each one of them was thinking only of the profit that he was to make. When those who were for going forward prevailed, everyone agreed, and preparations were put in hand, for we had decided to set out that night.

As soon as we had finished eating, the gong was sounded and we set out. We changed our route for fear of raiders, and made a detour through the desert. This change of route was to be a disaster for us. From the time that we set out from Murzuk travelling through the night we met no-one; nor did we hear any movement, until dawn found us near some great sand dunes which the wind had piled up. When we reached the vicinity of these dunes, the sun appeared and the caravan leader said that we should rest here and wait until the heat of the sun had abated before setting out again. We dismounted, and everyone took off his camel's saddle. We rested, and after we had drunk water we ate our food. We settled down in the place; those who wanted to walk did so; those who wanted to sleep, slept; those who wanted to read the Koran, did so; and those who wanted to talk, talked. Each one of us did as he pleased until the sun had passed its zenith.

While everyone went about his business, and all were completely off their guard, we suddenly heard shouting from the direction of our companions who had gone walking, and we saw them in the distance, running helter-skelter like a flock of Uda sheep.[1] Barely had we turned our glance towards the east when we saw something out there, jet black, like a storm cloud, rising up from the ground towards the sky, and making in our direction. For my part, I did not know what it was, but as for the others of our company, I saw each one begin to gather his loads together with cries of despair. I just stood still, staring, not knowing what was happening. Then barely had I lifted my head when I saw this thing in front of me, like a storm cloud. But it was no storm. It was the wind which had increased and turned into this. And in the wind there was nothing but sand. When the wind reached us I saw the whole place thrown into confusion, and I could distinguish nothing, let alone did I know where my companions were. I became confused, and lost all track of what was happening.

I ALONE ESCAPE AFTER THE SAND STORM

Not to make a long story of it, the wind did not begin to abate until a long time later, and then it began to drop a little. When my eyes could at last distinguish things around me, I looked out into the open desert, and I saw there was no-one; I was quite alone. And of the sand dunes beneath which we had halted, I saw not a sign.

1 The Udawa are migratory Fulani who breed a certain strain of long-legged sheep.

Then fear seized me, and in my heart I thought that my last hour had surely come. Then I thought of my master and the rest of our company, for in my heart I began to fear that the sand must have engulfed them all. I walked around calling Abdulkarim, but I heard no answer, nor even a sound, until I was tired. Then I sat down and burst into tears. There I remained until night fell. I lay down under God's open sky, but I could not even sleep.

When dawn came I got up and began once again to walk to and fro, in the hope that I might see some living thing. Not one single sign did I see, I just kept wandering about, not knowing in what direction I was going. Three days I spent thus, and then the little water which I had in my water-gourd was finished. I was parched with thirst, the sun was burning hot, and not a scrap of shelter was there. I couldn't even stand up, let alone walk about. I lay down, awaiting death.

On the fourth day, about the time of evening prayer, I was lying there when I heard a cry like that of a camel. My heart failed me. I raised my head, and then I saw far off in the distance a loaded camel making for where I was. I said, 'Truly, God is Almighty!' I simply gazed at it until it came up to me, sniffing at me. It stopped, I looked at it. Why, it was my own camel! Then I saw it kneel down in front of me, and I dragged myself forward until I reached it, seized the water skin, and drank. My senses returned to me, and I took a little food and ate it, and I gave thanks to God. I slept there together with the camel.

When dawn broke I felt strong. I packed up my things and mounted, and the camel stood up. I was wondering which direction I should take, when I realised that my camel had taken a road of his own accord. For my part, when I saw that, I did not interfere, but I just left him to continue on his way, until one day I began to catch sight of some date-palms in the distance. When we reached the place where these trees were, I saw that it was a large town. My camel went on until he brought me to the side of a water-hole, and here he stopped, and stood still. I got down off his back, drew some water, and gave it to him, and then I went to the foot of a tree, and sat down near to some caravan-travellers. I found them talking and heard them saying that on that day week, God willing, they would reach Birnin Kuka, in Bornu. They went on talking, and for my part, my heart was full of joy that I had found some people who were going to my own country.

Now we were sitting at the bottom of this tree, in the midst of our talk, when suddenly we heard shouting from within the town. Immediately afterwards we saw people running out. Before long we saw the houses go up in flames. We all stood up, and made ready to move off. We mounted our camels and stood over our loads. Hardly had we made ready than we saw a host of men with guns. On seeing them we scattered, each one taking whatever direction he thought would take him to safety. We began to gallop. The majority, when they began to gallop, made off in the direction from which they had come, that is to say, out into the desert. For my part, I sped off on my camel, and turned towards these armed men. I came up with them and passed them at a gallop. I raced on until I arrived at a big town with many baobab trees. I came to some compound and got down from my camel, with all my strength gone from my body.

The householder came out and said to me, 'Where have you come from?'

I said to him, 'We've been driven out of another town by some raiders.'

He replied, 'It must be some of Rabeh's men, who are fleeing here in disorder, after he himself was captured and killed by the French.'[1]

---

[1] Rabeh was the chief lieutenant of Sulaiman Pasha, the son of the famous slaver Zubair Pasha. Sulaiman Pasha rebelled against the government of Egypt, and was severely defeated. Rabeh took flight with the remnants of his forces and in 1878 began a series of raids on the tribes of Bahr al-Ghazal area. He pushed westward and attacked Bagirmi, Bornu, and Gobir, and threatened Sokoto, but was checked by the Sultan's forces. He turned back towards the east, and terrorised the area for some twenty-two years. He was eventually killed in a battle against the French in 1900.

I was not able to leave this town because my camel became sick. After six days in the place he died. Five days after his death I set out for my own country on foot. The days passed, until eventually God brought me safely to this town of yours, Rauta. Here I heard the news that Makau had died. I had no other relatives to go and see, so I settled here, teaching the Koran. So now you know the reason for my coming to your country.

Praise be to God. O God, Thou art the One to Whom we give our thanks. I pray the Lord to forgive us for those things which we have done, and those things which we shall do in the future. Lord God, drive away from us sorrow and the envy of enemies, and deliver us from the evil of this world and the next, Amen.